Damselfish

For Salma
shades of Canada
and Mexico !
Love,
Sue

Damselfish

a novel by

Susan Ouriou

Series Editor
Rhonda Bailey

National Library of Canada cataloguing in publication

Ouriou, Susan

Damselfish : a novel

(Tidelines)

ISBN 1-894852-05-2

I. Title. II. Series : Tidelines (Montréal, Québec).

PS8579.U74D35 2003   C813'.6   C2003-941072-2
PS9579.U74D35 2003

Legal Deposit: Third quarter 2003
National Library of Canada
Bibliothèque nationale du Québec

XYZ Publishing acknowledges the financial support our publishing program receives from the Canada Council for the Arts, the Book Publishing Industry Development Program (BPIDP) of the Department of Canadian Heritage, the ministère de la Culture et des Communications du Québec, and the Société de développement des entreprises culturelles.

All the characters in this book are fictional, and any resemblance to actual persons living or dead is purely coincidental.

Layout: Édiscript enr.
Cover design: Zirval Design
Cover painting: *Flying Downstream* (detail) by Susana Wald
Painting photographed by: Manu Sassoonian

Set in Bembo 12 on 14.
Printed and bound in Canada by Métrolitho
(Sherbrooke, Québec, Canada) in August 2003.

XYZ Publishing
1781 Saint Hubert Street
Montreal, Quebec H2L 3Z1
Tel: (514) 525-2170
Fax: (514) 525-7537
E-mail: info@xyzedit.qc.ca
Web site: www.xyzedit.qc.ca

Distributed by: Fitzhenry & Whiteside
195 Allstate Parkway
Markham, ON L3R 4T8
Customer Service, tel: (905) 477-9700
Toll free ordering, tel: 1-800-387-9776
Fax: 1-800-260-9777
E-mail: bookinfo@fitzhenry.ca

Katie and Dan,
I remember

For my husband Joël,
who needs no words

I

The Molson Export slogan played in my head, accompanying the rhythmic slap of the cards I laid down on the table. *X says it all.* One-two-three, slap. *X says it all.* Somehow I must have known that solitaire would be a big part of my new life when I brought the Molson Export deck from home.

I tipped back my bottle of beer – Dos Equis – and dislodged a grain of lime pulp from between my teeth. I liked Mexican beer better. Maybe two X's say it best.

For once luck was with me in my game of solitaire. Of the seven cards I'd laid face up to start with, three were aces. Luck doesn't visit me that often. Now all four aces were out, and the cards they'd been hiding were lining up under them like bottles of beer on a wall. I hadn't even had to cheat yet. I was still dealing the deck out by threes.

The woman staring down at me from my new and one-and-only made-in-Mexico painting was proof that luck could change. A woman, naked, seated pretzel-like with a giant bougainvillea, its colour a warm red, sprouting from her crotch. A few days ago I thought I had nothing to paint. A few days ago I thought flowers only grew in the ground. Meeting José had made me see it didn't have to be that way.

X says it all. A knock sounded at the door. I glanced up. José? No, he didn't know where I lived. Somehow, I'd forgotten that detail. Hard to believe, now. I'd promised to drop by at the market school on Monday. I'd make sure he got my address then. Or maybe even earlier.

I looked down at the deck of cards and back up as another knock sounded. Having someone at the door was a novelty. But so was a winning streak. Since arriving in Mexico City, I'd spent all my nights – well, all my nights but that one – alone in the apartment. I usually sat across from the flimsy curtains at my kitchen table, played solitaire, and watched the passing silhouettes of the hotel guests who shared a landing with me. Every night I fought the growing urge to knock on a door, any door, and join a lone traveller in his bed.

The apartments were tenements really, the hotel leaned to luxury and cachet. Mexico is like that: the mix of rich, poor, and in-betweens living side by side.

I kept telling myself one-night stands were not a good idea, but my body kept saying otherwise.

I should really answer that door.

I put the deck down, gave it a pat – don't go anywhere, we're on a roll – pushed my chair back, strode to the door, and pulled it wide. Then stood open-mouthed.

My sister. Faith. Here in Mexico. Or could I have been transported back to Montreal? I couldn't make sense of it – Quebec or Mexico? Sun or snow? Maybe I was losing my mind.

She laughed at my confusion. "Aren't you even going to say hi?"

We hugged, awkwardly. I didn't remember her being quite so round. I was a hugger, Faith wasn't. She always rationed me in my hugs: two a year. At Christmas and on my birthday. Was it my birthday then? No, despite the heat this wasn't July but October. And Christmas was still to come.

When I was filling out the grant application back home in Montreal, I'd imagined my move here as a chance to live and breathe art away from the distractions of everyday life. I'd imagined sleeping in my studio, rising from my mattress to my canvas, and munching on a burrito with a paintbrush in hand. But the studio wasn't anywhere near my apartment; it was a metro ride away in Coyoacán. The three other artists who worked there commuted from across Mexico City, too. They were all foreigners – one American, one Frenchman, and a Swiss, another woman – there on artists' grants like me. The others came mostly on the days when the model sat – the model I'd finally been able to paint. Our government contact talked of galleries to visit, conferences to address, exhibits to prepare, but as soon as he backed out the door his promises were forgotten.

I'd been keeping my days uselessly busy. I trotted out rusty Spanish to buy art supplies and groceries for my tiny fridge, spent hours and many days returning to offices to line up for a phone hookup and beg for the electricity to be turned on. I walked the streets, stored images, smells, and sounds, but in the studio my work wasn't going the way I'd imagined it from a continent away. I tried to force myself to transfer the images I was collecting to canvas, without much success – until the bougainvillea lady decided to sprout.

It had been impossible to paint what I couldn't understand. My eyes, my ears, my sense of touch were no good to me until I could translate their registers for myself. Everything outside me was opaque, deflecting my gaze right back at me. Almost everything.

Then again, it wasn't true that none of the images or sounds of Mexico were registering. It was Papi's voice, the familiar almost-forgotten tilt of his head from the back in a crowd, in the metro, that I heard and saw at every turn. Back home he'd never appeared to me, not once since the day he left ten years ago. Here, the sightings were torture in one way, but in another, a rush. The thought that he might be out there, that one day we might meet. To feel his presence where for so long there had been none.

Seeing my sister made me wonder whether the same unspoken longing had brought her here. The hope of a possible reunion with the father of our fatherland. Our father.

She looked as out of place as I'd felt since I got here. She was even more obviously gringoesque than I was: taller, broader, whiter. Her Mexican half didn't show. Was this what it had felt like for Papi in Quebec? Forever a stranger in a strange land?

"Why didn't you tell me you were coming? What are you doing here?"

Faith ignored my questions. As usual. "I was thinking of moving in."

That's when I noticed the suitcase at her feet. A big one. I looked from the suitcase to Faith in shock.

Faith backtracked ever so slightly, "Maybe to start with, you could just ask me inside."

I stood back and let her pass. I couldn't get my mind around what I'd just heard. My move to Mexico was supposed to be a new beginning. A fresh canvas. A time to figure myself out. Admittedly, nothing much had come of it so far. For me or my art or Papi. But what were the chances of any of that happening with my big sister – the ever-present big sister I'd just moved away from – hovering over me?

My expression must have held all the questions I couldn't seem to mouth. Faith and I gave up on words long ago. Or rather, we gave up on finding the words.

"You remember the new project I told you about before you left? The university finally gave me the go-ahead. They cut through all the red tape so I could leave right away."

She set the suitcase down and looked around. "It is kind of small here, isn't it?"

She turned back to me and let her hand light on my arm for a second. "Everything's been so last-minute. I thought I could crash here with you."

"But, Faith…"

She jumped in before I could say anything she'd want me to take back, "I'd help pay the rent."

"Why not just get your own place? The university would spring for it." Faith worked at McGill. In a research department – linguistics or philology – I could never get it straight.

"Well, there's a bit of a problem with funding. The money still has to be worked out."

I wondered what that meant exactly. And how many stories within stories I wasn't being told.

"I swear. I'll be out most of the time doing research, you won't have to worry about me getting in the way."

What could I say? And really, what did I want to say? I would never have thought it, but a city of twenty-two million strangers can be a pretty lonely place. Loneliness the predator, me the prey.

Things were getting better. Or had, and still could now that I'd met José, found the market school, and started painting again, but there remained all those endless hours after the sun went down.

"What about Marc?" I asked. Marc had been Faith's live-in for the past four years. Off and on. Every time she felt the need to show her life revolved around no man, they split up. But they always got back together again.

I liked men, but I'd never lived with just one man. I liked them best in the plural.

"He'll manage." Her tone was curt. "So, what do you say?"

I shrugged. I looked down at the kitchen table and at what might have been my best solitaire game ever. The cards slid back too easily into neat little piles. While I put the deck away, Faith opened her suitcase, pulled out a plastic Steinberg bag, and leaned against the door for balance while she took off first one shoe then the other, lined them up against the wall, and pulled out her slippers. Sensible slippers with support. I did notice with a hint of satisfaction that they were lined with fleece. I wondered how long it would be before Faith put them away never to take them out again. She'd discover that bare feet on cool linoleum was the only way to survive when the heat got bad.

Faith came to bed wearing her old T-shirt. The one she used to wear for chores around the apartment in Montreal. It was a faded purple with a rip high on the left-hand side and a stretched, deformed collar. The T-shirt-cum-nightie slipped off, baring one shoulder as she walked into the bedroom with her boom box under her arm. It reminded me of those Saturday mornings after I moved into the apartment with Faith and her boyfriend, once Mom had seen me through high school and taken off. Saturdays Faith wore that same shirt as she vacuumed, still half-asleep, her hair mussed, the firm, round slope of one shoulder or the other always exposed. She definitely filled the T-shirt out more than she used to.

She dragged her suitcase into the bedroom behind her, flipped back the top, pulled out a roll of paper towels, placed several sheets down on the floor then put both hands on either side of one neatly stacked pile of clothes then another and laid them against the wall. She pulled out one, two, three big black books – an encyclopedia – and some smaller what looked like guide books. She straightened my books on my rough pine board bookshelf, pausing for a second when she saw what they were. Papi's books of poems.

She set the boom box on the floor next to the bed then turned to face me, where I lay watching her still. "Want a back rub?" I hadn't had one for years now; from nightly occurrences when we were kids, they slowly tapered off after Papi left.

She checked the plug on the boom box she'd set down next to the bookcase while I rolled onto my stomach, my face in the pillow. I had no T-shirt to shed, the air was too stifling in my apartment to wear any clothes to bed. I could hear her slip a cassette into the tape deck and press start. Luba began to wail as my sister's hands touched my wrists. In one fluid motion, she ran her fingers from the upturned palms of my hands, along my elbows and inner arms, up over my shoulder blades, and into the hair at the base of my neck. I felt the familiar shiver of pleasure and gave a small sigh. Slowly she increased the pressure until she was kneading my muscles like a potter her clay, and the pleasure gave way to pain. Pain had never felt so good.

I started missing her touch before she had even stopped, just feeling the pressure ease off. But instead of tapping my shoulder to signal my time was up, Faith only lifted her hands to better centre them on either side of my spine. The gentle notes she began to play on either side of my vertebrae were her own Morse code, I remembered now. All these years later, her fingers still held the notes inside. I concentrated, picking out the tune, made easy this time by the tape she was accompanying. Faith and Luba. Both here to stay.

II

When I woke up late the next morning, Faith was not in bed. I found her sitting bolt upright in the kitchen, tapping her toes like a fiddle player, and waiting impatiently for our day to begin. I resigned myself to not getting over to see José that day. There was the orientation she wanted me to give her to the neighborhood, a dry run she wanted us to make to find the library where she'd be doing all her research, and a car rental place to visit where she could rent a car for the length of her stay. She didn't know yet that nothing gets done in a hurry in Mexico City, but she soon found out. Just as she found out that a car could be more of a nuisance than a convenience, somewhat along the lines of fleece-lined slippers and old T-shirts.

The car only lasted one night. We didn't get back to the apartment with it until close to dinnertime. I sat inside, waiting double-parked in the street as Faith ran up for the guidebook she wanted to take along for what she called our night out on the town.

I read the map, she drove. The car had no seat belts, something I should have remembered from the time we came to Mexico with Papi. Papi thought Canadians were crazy, so obsessed with saving ourselves. Buckle up, wear a helmet, cross on green, smokers outside, work up a sweat. All because we believed we were in control. Because we thought fate would turn a blind eye so long as we believed, so long as we had faith.

Faith. The story goes that my sister's name was a source of endless arguments between our parents. Finally, they decided Mom would be the one to choose for the firstborn and Papi the second. Papi always used to tease Mom that the name she picked was like just another seat belt. The origins of my name are much more murky but, from the little information either parent was ever willing to give out, Papi himself was hospitalized when I came into the world and not in a name-choosing mood. So Mom had to come up with another name for a baby girl. Hope. Maybe she felt fate needed a bit of a nudge.

Mexicans knew destiny spared no one. If your time was up, it was up. That was why every bus driver had a picture of the Virgin swinging from his rearview mirror, and every teenager learned the routine: key in the ignition, left foot on the clutch, shift into first, then give the sign of the cross. Only then did they step on the gas.

If I hadn't had to read the map for Faith, I would have felt safer with my eyes shut tight. We travelled down Paseo de la Reforma in one of eight lines of traffic while cars whipped from one lane to the next in front of us, turning without warning, honking. Pedestrians dodged the chaos. Faith wanted to take me to the pre-Columbian restaurant her guidebook billed as an authentic experience, a restaurant that served ants and maguey worms. As she drove, she told me more about the specialty, a delicacy – roasted ants poured onto a taco and smothered in hot sauce.

I'm not too big on ants. And I'm a useless navigator.

"For Christ's sake, Hope," she said. "Where am I supposed to turn?"

"How should I know?" I told her. "I can't even see the bloody signs."

She wanted to pull over and have me ask directions from a uniformed man. The one carrying a regulation rifle in his hands, the muzzle pointing straight at my head. I said no thank you, I'd rather drive on. We circled for over an hour, stuck by traffic in lanes that went nowhere. Somehow we finally ended up back on our own street and saw a car pulling out. We took its spot. Then walked back to my flat – our flat now – buying four greasy tacos from a vendor on the way. So much for a night on the town. Who wanted to eat ants anyway?

The money for the rental car would be better spent on another bed. But would it fit? If not, a fold-out couch for the front room. For Faith, of course.

Back home when we were little, we'd start out in one bed taking turns at back rubs, then go off to our own beds to sleep. Sometimes at night, though, when I was six or seven, I'd have nightmares: under-the-bed long-limbed monsters whose disembodied voices drowned out my own. I'd jump out of bed, quickly before my ankles were grabbed by one of those long arms, and crawl in with Faith. I couldn't snuggle close, she hated to be mauled, so I'd just graze her arm with my finger or let my toe rest on her calf. Enough to feel her force field billow up around me, one my nightmares couldn't break through. Even after Papi left, she'd allow me that.

But I was twenty-four now, she was twenty-six, and the temperature was twenty-two. Sleeping with my sister was not what it used to be.

She didn't wake up early the following morning when I slipped out of bed. I took my clothes into the next room – the only other room to be exact, not counting the bathroom. It looked a little less bare now with Faith's laptop on the table and her boom box on the bookcase we'd moved out from the bedroom to make way for her suitcase. I'd bought the bookcase in the street early on, from a peddler who carried the rough pine boards nailed haphazardly into a bookshelf-like shape on his back. The case now held what amounted to an actual collection of books. It was a good thing Faith hadn't brought the whole twenty-some volume Britannica though.

I patted the back pocket of my jeans. The used metro ticket that José had written his address on was still there. I was finally going to go back to his place, the apartment I'd seen just the once. I felt a sudden rush of heat. What was I embarrassed about, I hadn't been that drunk. But still, in the cold light of day… Anyway, I wasn't going there to talk about the other night. This was about my promise to volunteer at the market school. Today was Monday, the day I'd said I would come. Now I'd have to cancel out because of Faith and her other plans.

The first time I stumbled on the market school some two weeks before, it was by sheer accident. Out of total frustration – with my inability to paint, draw or find some other way, any other way, to translate my new life to canvas – I abandoned my paintbrush and easel in the Coyoacán studio and went out to clear my head.

My senses were already overloaded enough so I decided to skirt the marketplace with its spices, chilies, fishmongers' shrieks, shoppers trying to make their orders heard above the din, and strangers jostling, unseeing. I vaguely remembered a park out back, so I bypassed the mercado and made for the other side.

Small children were sprawled on the ground between the benches in the middle of the park. I could see the dirt-patterned soles of their bare feet. Each was huddled over a piece of paper, each held a stubby pencil. A man walked among them. He looked to be about my age, taller than me but slight. He wore a colourful woven belt around his jeans and a navy blue shirt with long sleeves, its cuffs rolled halfway up his forearms. His head bent to look at the papers on the ground. Every once in a while he knelt down to speak to a child. A young teen, small for his age, shoulders bowed, followed the man as he walked from child to child. I was struck by the contrast with the cocky adolescents I remembered from back home, 20 below but shoulders back like peacocks to show off their unzipped winter parkas and their eff-you attitude to the cold.

As I drew closer, the man raised his head and looked at me with eyes that beckoned me in instead of reflecting me out.

I felt I had to say something. I looked down at the little girl and the drawing she was working on

"Son pájaros en el cielo, no?" Six black Vs in a sky shot through with colour; not one crayon shade had been left out. The little girl bit her lip.

"De España?" the man asked. My lisp, so apparent back home, was taken for a Spaniard's accent here – thielo instead of sielo – not some physical blight.

"No, Canadá."

He turned to the young teen behind him. "Guillermo, see, someone to practise English with. Practicar." The boy tilted his head and smiled shyly. Another small boy called out to the man from a bench on the far side. "José," he said. The man looked, waved, turned back to me, reached out his hand, and welcomed me with his eyes. I extended my hand, a simple handshake, and met his gaze. Long enough to let me know I wanted to go back.

I'd gone back by almost every weekday since, either morning or afternoon. Since I wasn't painting anyway it didn't make any sense to spend all day stuck in front of my easel. Seeing José again did make sense.

Mornings were when the children dropped by the in-market school – they actually worked at the market, some of them as young as four – whenever they had some free time or wanted a break. That was when José, who had been hired

by the city to start up such a school, had the use of a space
donated by the merchants, which he'd filled with second-
hand desks and books and blackboards. Afternoons, he took
them wherever he could, usually the park. The children or
their parents, if they had any, couldn't afford the books and
supplies to go to the public school so that was why the city
had subsidized José to school the children where they
worked.

That afternoon last week at the marketplace, it was José's
suggestion that we get together afterwards. That was how the
evening started, too – just the two of us getting together for
a drink. Discovering we lived not far apart, he a few metro
stops before mine. Each of us going home to change and
grab a bite to eat, meeting at a bar halfway between our two
places at ten o'clock. In the bar, it was harder to keep up the
flow of conversation, both of us used to the constant inter-
ruptions from the market kids. I felt us move into that awkward space where spoken words falter and body language
hasn't yet picked up the slack. That's when I always start to
drink too much. During one of the longer pauses, as we
avoided each other's eyes, José said, "Do you like to dance?"

I drained my mug. "Uh, I guess so."

"The discoteca is just down the street."

Somehow this felt like an admission of failure, but I nodded and tried to smile.

José was a gifted dancer, thanks, as he told me, to weekly
trips as a teen from his village to neighbouring town dances.
A dedicated dancer, too. In his eyes, dancing and drinking
just didn't mix. He might have been right. Sometimes I
couldn't tell whether the spinning in my head and the
churning in my stomach came from the dancing or the beer.
Eventually, like José, I switched to orange juice, afraid that
otherwise I wouldn't be able to keep up.

At first, the awkwardness of conversation carried on into
the dance. I didn't know what messages his hand was meant

to convey on my back while we jived or just how to find the beat. But José smiled encouragement and kept guiding me in, out, round, back. We were both sweating, the crowd around us pulsing, my breath ragged from exertion when the tempo changed, slowed to a waltz.

Enveloped in music, black light, and body heat, pelvis against pelvis, hands creeping from waist to hips to flanks, our dialogue took off. A discoteca was no longer the place for us. Thankfully, José's apartment was nice and close.

The eyes of the woman-of-the-sprouting-crotch followed me. My very first paintings when I majored in art in college – CEGEP – were images of sleds, severed limbs and hearts, broken, bleeding, beating still in the coldest oils I could find. I tired of their garishness though and slowly began to favour watercolours and charcoal drawings of empty chairs, doors ajar, half-eaten meals, and abandoned closets of clothes, trying to convey the violence of the quotidian through the act of watering down. Or at least, that's how the review committee phrased it when they awarded me my grant.

This last woman I'd created in warm oils was present like none other. Her eyes spoke of the here and now.

I dressed in one minute flat, a specialty of mine, then stepped outside, shut the door, and took the two flights down.

I was glad José's apartment was within walking distance. This early in the morning, there was no one on my street. A city of 22 million, and no one in sight. This was the time of day, the only one, when I felt Mexico City was a living being that could some day be a friend.

I stopped in front of the panadería and hesitated. Maybe I should bring something along. The sweet smell of bread drew me inside. I wandered up and down each aisle, six in all, finding the staggering selection of breads, cakes, and desserts at this early hour almost too much. I picked out three panques and three buns with my metal tongs, and carried the tray to the cash register to be rung in. I had the girl put one of the buns and one of the panques in a bag. For Faith later, after José.

Past the panadería, I turned right, so busy communing with the heart of the city that I just about crushed a dead sparrow lying at my feet.

It wasn't the only one. There were four of them in a circle on the sidewalk. I bent and touched the sparrow I'd almost crushed. Its body was plump, its feathers sleek. No teeth marks, no prowling cat. It almost looked asleep.

I looked up through the tree branches to the grey-washed sky above. Was this a sign? At home, the thought wouldn't have crossed my mind, but here signs existed. An Aztec curse, a father's ghost.

In Mexico I was ready to believe that people really did commune with the spirits or sprout bougainvillea inside body folds.

The scrape of metal against concrete announced a street sweeper shuffling toward me – shirttails hanging, pants ripped at the knee, dragging a twig broom behind him, a long-handled dust pan in his hand, and a garbage bag looped at his side. He stopped and looked down at the sparrows.

"Otros!" he grumbled. "Qué bárbaro! Qué noche aquella!"

He eased in front of me and started sweeping the birds up with his broom. I walked away, not wanting to see sparrows turned to waste. Two blocks farther down I found the address that matched the one on the metro ticket. I didn't recognize the building in the daylight.

José must have been sound asleep. He looked rumpled and warm. His eyes were as much a dark welcome in near-sleep as awake. His chest was bare, and his jeans hung low on his hips without the woven belt to hold them up.

I forgot my excuse for being there. I just held out the buns, wrapped in tissue folded like a scarf.

"Qué onda!" he said.

The first time I heard that greeting was in the park. I thought he said Qué honda, meaning how's my Honda doing. I looked around for a motorbike lying nearby. But I learned it meant how's it going. Now, here, though, it meant, Isn't this great. In the little time I'd known him, José had already taught me the expressions of a younger generation, words Papi never knew.

"Hi," I finally said, remembering. "I'm sorry. It really is early, isn't it? It's just... I wanted to catch you before you left to tell you I can't help out... not today, but..."

"What's this?" José seemed more interested in my package than any explanation I could stammer out.

"Oh these, I thought you might like some..."

"You thought right."

He stepped closer to take the package from my outstreched hands and shut the door behind me.

"I'm sorry if I woke you up. I wasn't thinking. I should have come later. It's just, my sister's shown up, and I'll probably have to spend the day with her today, maybe even tomorrow too, which is why I thought I'd better come by, to tell you that I can't..."

José set the package down. "I'm not that hungry yet. You?"

"No." Not that kind of hungry. Knock-on-a-stranger's-door hungry, yes.

I'd come to the right place. He was warm. I could feel the heat of his chest, his hips, and his mouth through my tank top and jeans. Later, when his hands slid under my top and up, I could feel the soft trail of hair leading from his navel down. José's hands reached along my ribs and stopped when they encountered not material but flesh.

I pulled back slightly. "I don't believe in bras," I said.

"Me neither," he said as my top came off.

∿

Later in his bed I confessed, "Sex is my favourite sport."

"Then you're my favourite jock," José replied.

I laughed, José put his hands on either side of my head. "What's the Spanish for jock?" I asked even as he touched his tongue to my eyelids and turned my head in his hands. He didn't answer.

José, Josecito, Pepe, Pepito, Pepillo, who knows, why not mi amor, amor mío someday. What better language for the making of love than his?

He slid his thumbs to my throat, stroked the lump centred there, whispered, "Manzana for apple," glided to his knees, murmured, "And now for the forbidden fruit."

∿

I rolled onto my side, my head at José's feet. Traced a line along his calf, parting gentle hairs with my nail. In slow motion I traced and watched, reflexes drugged by sex. Thought to myself, he has to go to work. "So tell me, what's so forbidden?"

José raised himself on one elbow, cast a glance at his travel clock, reached across, stroked a breast, my Venus mound, my ass. I noticed, detached, as my nipples grew hard again. "Not these, or this, or this. All of it. All of you. Gringa's the forbidden fruit."

"Gringa." Funny how the words to describe me multiplied. Baby, girl, sister, daughter, woman, lover. Kid, student, painter. Anglo, Canadian, and now this. Gringa. "I am half-Mexican, remember. Besides, Gringa's for Americans."

"Wrong again. We're the Americans, all of us Latinos to the south. Gringos are North American, that means you too."

"Not true. Canadians never came in uniform to invade Mexico. Those are the greens the Mexicans wanted to see go."

"Okay, okay, you win. How about I give you your prize?"

But there was something I still wanted to know. "So why are we, why am I forbidden?"

"Santos, you ask a lot of questions." He twirled around to point in my direction, dropped his legs over the side of the bed. "Here, I'll show you." He rummaged next to him on the top of the desk, the only other piece of furniture in his room. "Look at this."

He'd grabbed a magazine, flipped it open to an ad, full page. A picture of a milk carton stamped Made in U.S.A. Underneath was the caption "No sean malinchistas. Digan no al TLC." Don't be Malinchistas. Say no to the TLC.

"TLC. That's the free trade agreement Mexico's negotiating with Canada and the U.S., right?" José nodded. Back home, I'd had a union button handed to me on the same agreement. It said, Free Canada – Trade Mulroney. "Who's Malinche?"

"Ever heard of Doña Marina? Cortés's interpreter."

"Uh-huh."

"That's her. The one who sold out. Defected to the other side. La Malinche was the name the natives gave her. Any of us who go to the other side, to the gringos, we call them Malinchistas. Looks like I'm going to be a Malinchista for a while."

For a while. I said the only thing that came to mind. "In English, TLC stands for tender loving care."

I walked him to the metro, broken crates, banana peels, and cigarette butts littering the gutters at our feet. I remembered the street sweeper, told José.

"Happens all the time. In the middle of the night. The pockets of smog get so bad the birds can't breathe. They fall from the trees, and we wake up to them the next day. A new spot every time. Here today, a month from now thirty blocks further down. The air moves in mysterious ways."

He didn't notice my slight shudder.

III

After saying goodbye at the metro – both of us too awkward out in the open, too tentative, to kiss – I wanted to relive the morning with José, but the sparrows kept intruding. I walked slowly, not wanting to imagine birds toppling from branches, wings folded, never to unfurl for one last flight. I realized I couldn't be any part of the poisoned air.

There was only one solution. I would tell Faith the car was out. There was no way I'd add to the exhaust in the air that kept birds raining from the sky. I wasn't as sure what Faith's reaction would be. Well, actually, I was. Faith always told me that I think in headlines, that I'm the melodrama queen. I still remembered her reaction the day I decided to quit eating mammals. I was living with her and Marc then. After Mom left for Mexico.

Mammals, not meat. Because of a terrible dream I had. In my dream, we made a huge bonfire – Faith, Mom, and I – at first throwing on wooden crates, branches of trees, and book after book after book, some of them bearing Papi's name, until they were all gone. Then we threw a donkey, a pig, a calf, and a goat – mammals all – into the flame-ringed pit. Not one gave a cry, a squeal, or a scream. Their cries, squeals, or screams were sucked away by the ring of flames like molecules of oxygen. Worst of all, the fire created a

vacuum in me. I watched and felt nothing, there was nothing left to feel. The vacuum frightened me more than the
sacrificial act.

No other nightmare had ever made me feel that much
fear before, not as a kid in my bed alone, not even during the
long nights after Papi left. I had to listen to what the dream
was telling me.

Faith's reaction? "Mammals, you've given up mammals!
So, like, you're a non-mammalian now? Can't you just be a
vegetarian like everyone else?"

I expected more or less of the same when I told her
about the birds and the car. Faith accusing, like there was
something wrong with not being like everyone else. Like she
had something better to offer. And that wasn't all. If she did
agree to give up the car, she would probably figure this got
her out of the promise she made last night to come with me
the weekend after next. Mom had been back to Canada
seven times in the past seven years, but neither Faith nor I
had ever been down to see where she lived in Cuernavaca.
I'd told Mom before Faith arrived that I would go down one
weekend to visit her. She suggested a date to coincide with
one of her vacation breaks, one that would give me enough
time to settle in to the big city first. She mentioned us going
together to her friends' beach house, on the ocean, once
she'd shown me the place she now called home. "You could
tack some days onto the end of your stay in Mexico to make
up for the few days you spend with me." Now Faith was part
of that plan.

Faith thought of the hitch right away. "Where does that
put Cuernavaca? How do you think we're going to drive
down?"

"I didn't have a car when I told Mom I'd go to see her.
There are buses you know." Then I had an idea. Another
excuse. "Maybe José could give us a ride down. He mentioned he was planning on driving down to be with his fam-

ily for the Day of the Dead. Cuernavaca is on the way to his village down by Tehuacán."

"Who's José? And whoever he is, doesn't his car pollute the same as this one? What about your sacred principles?"

"But he only drives it for emergencies or trips outside the city."

I was like that, my principles easily swayed. Not like Papi. I believed Papi's leaving us had something to do with his principles coming first. Principles linked to a poet's obligations to put his art above all else and to a man's obligation to be free. A father's obligation got in the way and came between the other two. I couldn't help wishing his principles came last.

When I decided to cut out meat, I did it the real vegetarian way at first. I thought I could go whole hog – wrong expression that – and cut out all living creatures. But I was so hungry all the time! And I kept losing weight. At my skinniest, one of Papi's hugs would have crushed me.

I didn't know what to do. Then I got to thinking about my dream. About the animals we threw into the fire – a goat, a pig, a donkey – mammals only. So that's what my vision meant.

I didn't know yet where falling sparrows came in.

"You didn't answer my first question. Who is this José anyway?" Faith asked. "How much do you know about him?"

"For Christ's sake, how much do I know about anyone? You, for example? You're my sister, what more is there to tell? And he's my… he's my lover, that's all you need to know." I liked the feel of the word *lover* on my tongue. So much better than the alternatives. And true, technically. "He's a painter too, a fingerpainter. And a potter, a woodsmith, and a whiz at glue guns. Whatever it takes. He and a part-time social worker run the informal school for the children who work in the market. I've started helping – teaching reading and writing, maybe a bit of English, too – if I'm there in the morning when they have the classroom. If I go in the afternoon I help with crafts outside."

Faith had her own thoughts on the whole idea, but I was already busy planning how to ask José, glad for this new excuse to see him, so I let her words pass me by.

IV

I had a vice, a secret sin. I read other people's diaries, letters, notes to themselves. The words *Do not open*, *Private*,
Confidential, *Top Secret*, *For addressee's eyes only* were an open
invitation to me. Not that I was spying. A spy gathered
information to use against others. All I wanted was a
glimpse behind the masks and the images people projected.
Looking for answers to questions I hadn't yet figured out
how to ask.

It was Faith's doing actually. One day, when we were living together in Montreal after Mom left – Papi was already
long gone – I came home from CEGEP feeling extra sorry
for myself: Little Orphan Annie having to live with her bossy
older sister and her sister's boyfriend. I took a cooler out of
the fridge and plunked down on the couch to watch TV,
anything to drown out the self-pity. But Faith's notebook –
which I took for her coursework – was lying open on the
coffee table. I picked it up out of sheer boredom. Instead of
a linguistic treatise, I saw she'd written her self. Her anger at
Mom. Her frustration with sisterdom. I caught glimpses of
myself. It was too late. I couldn't help it. For the first time in
a long time, I didn't feel alone.

That was the only time Faith ever left her book lying out
in plain view, but the damage was done. I was hooked. All
that week, I kept sneaking into her bedroom for a peek

whenever she was out. The journal kept moving around, from her bedside table, to under the mattress, then hidden in a stack of books. But I always found it. That Saturday, she confronted me, holding up a strand of hair. "You little snoop," she said, "You've been reading my journal."

I'd always found the best response to any attack is counterattack. "What do you expect when you leave it lying around for anyone to see?"

"Don't give me that."

I did have the grace to blush, I think. Ever since, Faith had gone to incredible lengths to hide her journal. And I had to be extra careful about putting back any strands of hair, nail clippings, or pieces of fluff whenever I rooted it out.

This time I hadn't set out to pry. It was all because of the cockroaches. I couldn't stand them anymore. I was determined to find out where they were coming from before we left for Cuernavaca.

Every night we had to spray for those damn insects – I felt my lungs shrivel a little more each time – and every morning there were six or seven big new ones succumbing on the floor. I couldn't imagine coming home to several days' worth. Actually, I could. Which was why I decided to act.

My idea was to find their gateways into our flat and plant Raid inside. Yes, I valued the gift of life. In mammals, birds, and humans. Not in cockroaches. Not yet. Maybe someday I'd convert to Jainism, become a monk, and wear a gag so no flying creature's life could come to a brutal end in my mouth. I'd live on water and air. But not yet.

The bathroom was first on my list. All that damp made it a hothouse for bugs.

I found a broken tile just under the sink, with the bottom right-hand corner missing. The perfect size for a cockroach to squeeze through. With my bent knife – not much choice there since in my bargain apartment every chair wobbled, the table had a gimpy leg, forks were missing tines, plates were cracked, and knives were bent – I started to pry the tile from the wall. I was surprised at how easily it came off.

No cockroaches skittered away in the wavering light of my flashlight, but a gleaming something winked back at me – a plastic bag dangling out of a broken pipe. I counted to four then gingerly reached in and pulled it out.

Inside were several looseleaf sheets rolled into a tube. I saw Faith's writing on the top sheet and a date. To think I hadn't even been looking.

October 29, 1993

I was right! Nahuatl makes the perfect code! Who needs numbers and signs!

Key to code – keep any possibility of meaning from potential decoders – refer to reality no one knows exists (1st letters of Nahuatl words for most exotic Mexican flora and fauna = alphabet. Nahuatl the language of metaphor: white – izta-c – means 'like salt,' black – tlil-ti-c – 'like ink.' Endless poss. for combinations!)

Difficulties – the 35 dialects in modern Nahuatl. So much to learn!

I never thought Faith would be the kind to use exclamation marks. And for what? A bunch of foreign letters and words. The stuff of Faith's work was the forcing, bending, and twisting of words into unnatural, indecipherable codes; the stuff of my work was play – colours and textures that I scooped up and plastered on, not knowing precisely what hue or shape each blob would form. I never realized Faith might see her work as play, too. I skipped the code part and flipped to the next entry.

October 31, 1993

Mexico = Makesicko. Feel like throwing up most of the time. Losing
weight. No more Gordita, dreaded Papi nickname. Said it meant
sweetheart, not little fat one. I'm not so sure.

Found a tutor. Kiko's his name. Instant rapport.

Hope still looking for excuses not to paint: boyfriend, street kids,
reading bios, copying quotes. Overheard her on the phone with Mom
making plans for our trip and telling her she is a liver first, a painter
second. Hope should call herself a kidney while she's at it!

Ouch. Prying had its drawbacks.

She was wrong anyway. Already in the short time since
that first painting, I'd done several quick studies in charcoal
and ink. I was experimenting with the introduction of new
colours to my oil palette, the vivid colours of Mexico.
Helping at the market with the children was actually feed-
ing my work, too; the crafts, for me, were a new exploration
of old materials. And I'd taken a few bios of artists out the
day I showed Faith the way to the library: Frida Kahlo,
Georgia O'Keeffe, Debora Arango. She was the one who
said a nude is a landscape in human flesh. Oh, and La
Malinche. But she wasn't an artist. I was just curious. Plus, I
was going to be able to teach José something now. That
Malinche wasn't a traitor, not really. That she's the mother of
the majority of today's Mexican people, her child the first
mestizo – mixed blood – and that my blood is as mixed as
the rest. And how did Faith know I'd been keeping a record
of my favourite quotes?

Even when she was absent, she had the knack. I felt like
I'd been caught in the bathroom playing cockroach killer and
amateur spy when the studio was where I should really be at.

I rolled the sheets back together, slipped them into the

plastic bag, and pushed it back into the recess, shining the light first just in case. Faith would never know. Meanwhile, I might actually have to hide my quote book.

V

Faith's retching filled my ears and nose. We'd pulled off the road. José was standing next to the car and looking over the roof while I stood next to Faith on the other side, holding her forehead as she doubled over, all her weight pushing against my hand. This was a first for us. Back in Montreal, during my CEGEP years, I was always the one down on my knees hugging the toilet bowl, Faith's hand supporting me. Of course, mine was always due to too much Baby Duck, too many rum and Cokes, or a record night of beer chugging. Like today, my warm beer to give me courage for the reunion. Faith never over-indulged, over-imbibed, over-anything that I knew of. Always in such control.

It wasn't like she was one to get carsick either. That too was my specialty on our yearly holidays, trips across the entire breadth of the country (to become true Canadians we had to know the whole of Canada, Papi said. Papi never did anything by half measures) or, on one occasion, all the way back to Mexico. On the first day of driving, we'd inevitably have to stop by the side of the road at some point for me to throw up. That was on good days, when Papi managed to find a place to pull over soon enough. Faith hated it when he didn't make it in time. I was too far gone to care.

On our first night out, the ritual was always the same. Vacations, Mom decreed, were her time off from mothering,

so Papi washed my matted hair – somehow I never remembered until the second day to tie my hair back – in whatever
cheap motel room we'd managed to find, always, again, at
Mom's insistence. Left to his own devices, I think Papi would
have driven through the night. We called it being hyper.
In the moisture-sucking prairie provinces, on top of the
upchucking, my nose would start to bleed and keep on
bleeding for days.

Papi didn't seem to mind the vomit or the blood or the
dust. He took delight in helping me make soap-beehive hair-
dos, shampooed French buns, spikes on either side of my
head, then he'd hold the mirror up for me to admire our cre-
ations or fly into uncontrollable fits of laughter. Afterwards,
my favourite part, two parts pain to three parts bliss, I'd stand
shivering between his knees, one towel wrapped tight
around me, another in his hands, while he attacked my hair,
wringing every last drop of water out. He always rubbed too
hard, but the pleasure was never less than the pain.

I wondered if poets ever stopped to consider the pain or
pleasure they wreaked on their muse. Not that the pain was
Papi's fault, he just didn't know his own strength.

That's what holidays were, frequent pit stops, strong
thighs holding me upright as stronger hands buffeted my
scalp, a Grand Prix family on the move. Until Papi left.

We were on the crest of a hill. In the valley below lay
Cuernavaca, the City of Eternal Spring instead of eternal
pollution. The sky was blue, not the grey haze of Mexico
City, and the space above the car hood shimmered in the
heat. We could actually see the volcano el Popo, which José
said would be visible from Mexico City too if we ever had a
day without smog. Together he called el Popo and the dormant volcano beside it the Sleeping Woman, said each one of

the four peaks was named after a part of her body. I tried to focus on the volcanoes, breathe in clean air, and block my ears to sick-making heaves. José was right, the four mountain peaks did look like a woman asleep.

In art, to anticipate is to lose the truth of the movement, the gesture, the landscape, all the telling details. I had anticipated too long and too hard this trip, seeing my mother in a home I'd never known, imagining the three women of our family finally joining forces to track down a missing father and husband in his homeland. Now, instead, I concentrated on the distant volcano.

Faith stopped heaving. Her head – clammy not hot – lay heavy on my hand. I tried to imagine what could have brought this on, whether Faith said anything or gave any sign before her strangled plea for José to pull over.

José was into what must be his highway driving mode. Much more relaxing than his kamikaze city style. Faith hadn't been taking part in our conversation. I thought she'd dozed off in the back seat. It was as though José and I were alone in the car.

"When did you last see your parents?" I asked as we drove.

"My mother. My father died two years ago."

"Oh, I'm sorry."

José shrugged. "We weren't that close." The tone of his voice seemed to contradict his shrug. I waited.

José glanced over, put both hands on the wheel. "It felt like I spent most of his last few years trying to connect. The grown son he'd imagined would have stayed close to home, worked the land with him or, at the most, got a job in one of the water-bottling factories nearby. That son wasn't me. He didn't get it, what I was doing, who I am, what I'd become. We were both disappointed all the time. We quit trying. It got so I started finding excuses to stay in the city. Then he died. At least I made it back before the end. Anyway, this is one of the few holidays my mother insists on me driving down for." A pause. "Families, huh."

I watched the way he crossed one hand over the other as he turned the wheel. Switched from one topic to the next. "I guess I'd better explain how you and Faith can get around Cuernavaca. You'll be minus a chauffeur once I've gone."

I got the message. The subject of families was closed.

"It's easy to get around the city, just hop a bus, they call them rutas, for two pesos and you'll be able to go just about anywhere. Out to the San Antonio hacienda that Cortés built. Or to Tepoztlán, you'll have to go there, just outside Cuernavaca. A great hike to the top to a tiny pyramid that marks a sacred site. Worshippers go up there to watch the sun rise and pray for the gods' intervention."

"People still believe in all that?"

José looked over at me, even slowed down a little. "Well, yeah. Why not? What do you believe in?"

That was when Faith called out, "You've got to pull over. I'm going to be sick." I didn't have time to say what I believed. Even less to decide if I did.

Thanks to an old sink behind a gas station, Faith was sort of cleaned up by the time we reached Mom's place. The wrought-iron gate where José let us off led to the villa where her employers and landlords must live, the ones who ran the language school she worked in. The swimming pool, bougainvillea, mango, and banana trees we glimpsed from the road must belong to them as well. As must the broken Coke bottles glued to the top of the gate and along the fence, their jagged edges forming a bizarre frame.

She appeared in the door of a two-storey apartment block down the driveway from the villa, greying hair pulled back into a sloppy bun, loose strands escaping around her

face. I had a flashback: Mom standing in more or less the
same position at the foot of another hill in Montreal, one
covered in snow.

I waved. She smiled, waved back, started up the drive.
Her breasts were heavier now than they were those many
years ago, but her waist still indented slightly above generous
hips – just like Faith's. Compared to the two of them and
Papi, I'd always been out of place. Skinny, curveless me.

"I was starting to get worried," she called out to us.
"You're late."

I certainly wouldn't be the one to tell her why. Mom
tended to imagine the worst ever since Papi disappeared.

The day before Papi left, Mom stood at the bottom of
Mont-Royal, just like she stood at the foot of this rise, while
the three of us – Papi, Faith, and I – trudged to the top
above Beaver Lake dragging the crazy carpet behind. Once
there, Papi lay stomach down – mouth down as the
Mexicans say – toes digging into the snow, with Faith boca
abajo on him because she was the oldest and the biggest and
me on top of the two of them. In one motion, Papi pushed
off.

Papi was a big man, thick bones, solid muscle, with a bit
of a paunch. Faith took after him, except for the paunch. The
two of them like two sturdy cushions under my bony frame,
softening the bumps and hollows we hit. It never got that
good again.

That day, ten years ago – me fourteen, Faith sixteen – we
must have looked bizarre, too old for kids' games but shooting down the hill anyway. Racing after a childhood.

Faith gave a gasp on the first bump as my body floated
up and slammed back into hers. Wind chomped at the top of
my head and along my back. Crystals of snow flew up from
the toboggan runners and burnt my tongue.

That time, Papi didn't whoop and sing, or even gasp and
grunt. Just kept his head to the sled as we hurtled down. Like

he was trapped between the lash of wind, the crunch of snow, and his daughters' weight.

I saw the approaching sled.

I tried to shout, but my voice – high and breathy at the best of times – was swallowed by the wind.

Our path veered. We headed for the trees along the sides, on target for the spear of a branch. I tucked my chin, closed my eyes, and felt the scratch of a twig on my cheek.

I raised my head and saw we were headed straight down the hill now, on a collision course with Mom. She waved, hair and scarf whipped by wind, her body standing firm, smiling as we plummeted down. God, couldn't she see? The ride from hell, and she did nothing but smile. No wonder she named us Faith and Hope; she wasn't capable of imagining anything else.

At the last minute, Papi put his head up, threw his arm to the side, and changed the course of our run. Mom kept waving and smiling, pretending everything was all right.

The next day Papi left. Without saying a word. Then or now.

They say Mont-Royal is a volcano, supposedly extinct. But I swear I have felt its rumblings ever since.

Papi's leaving was as physical as a sled broadsiding Mom where she stood. From out of nowhere, she said. When she could have seen it coming. So could I if I'd only read the last poems he'd typed: "The Forgotten Lines," "Intimacy Untold," "Animal of Despair." The words he never spoke that I might have heard if I'd read them in time. He painted word pictures, now I tried to bring them to life with a graphite pencil or a brush. Both of us looking for what could have been, what wasn't, and the wide spaces in between.

So many words still left unspoken. As many after his departure as before, if not more. Meaningless words were the only ones uttered, not the words that mattered most. Why did he go? Where had he gone? For how long?

The only thing I knew for sure was that ever since that day, Mom had learned to fear the worst, as if making up for lost time. It was better for everyone if we kept Faith's spell of sickness quiet. Our secret.

We all smiled awkwardly as Mom walked up the slope, fumbled with the lock and chain, and swung the gate open.

She came up to me, kissed my cheek once, turned to Faith, and brushed her cheek as well. I held my breath. She didn't seem to notice Faith's still-pallid skin, red-ringed eyes, or limp hair. She was too busy turning to José with a questioning look.

"Mom, this is José Molinar, a friend. José, my mother, Ramona Alder."

She smiled and shook his hand. The calculations had already begun. How much of a friend? How long? Where from? "Won't you come in?"

"Gracias, but no. I'll leave you to your homecoming. Better without an intruder."

Homecoming. Strange home considering I'd never been here before. The last home I had with Mom was in Montreal. The one the three of us stayed on in after Papi left; a mother and two teenage girls, not the perfect mix. But then Faith moved out with her boyfriend and I reached college-age and Mom decided to start over again. Now I wondered if she and I would ever catch up on that time she had missed between my teenhood and womanhood.

José had mentioned an intrusion, too. There could be no intrusion when he had been invited in. But Mom didn't insist, her attention was already turning back to Faith and me. So I didn't insist either. Although I wanted to.

José opened the trunk and held out Faith's suitcase and my backpack. Faith didn't even make a show of taking charge, she must really be sick. I hoped Mom didn't notice. She'd have Faith at death's door in no time. José came close, his arm brushing mine as he handed over the bags. His touch was a magnet to my skin, the prick of iron shavings coming to life. I wanted to drop the bags, grab his neck, and give in to the pull. I didn't. He kissed me lightly, gripped Mom's hand, then Faith's with a pat on her shoulder, and climbed back into the car. "Give me a call from the bus station when you get back." He stared pointedly at Faith, who still looked like she was having trouble finding the strength to stand straight. "I can give the two of you a lift." I watched him drive off as my mother and sister started walking down the rise.

Mom gave us a whirlwind tour of her apartment, then over to the villa, where we had to climb a ladder attached to the outer wall to our guest room, actually the maid's room, a concrete box perched on the top of the flat roof. Dozens of birds chirped from among the leaves of a tall mango tree whose top hugged the outer wall of the box which was actually a bedroom that had no door, just two openings, one the doorway, the other a window entirely open to the elements, and one bunk bed. The only other furnishings were an ironing board and a wooden chair piled high with clothes. I'd thought Mom's apartment looked spartan, this was beyond belief.

"The dueños are between maids right now. Their last girl left, so they offered to let you two sleep here. Otherwise, we'd have had to string up two hammocks in my place."

"I can see why she left," I remarked. I tried to catch Faith's eye, but she was still winded from the climb and didn't notice. She looked almost grey in this light. Mom just shrugged.

The landlady and landlord were at their front door as we climbed back down the ladder. Both were of a stocky build but dressed for a younger, slimmer age. He wore an open-necked shirt and jeans, she a long white T-shirt over black leggings. The woman came over first, smiled, and shook our hands. Mom pulled her aside as her husband stepped up to greet Faith and me. "¡Qué *linda* familia! ¡Qué placer *infinito* es encontrarles a las hijas de nuestra *gran* amiga! Soy Miguel." I smiled in spite of myself. Somehow, after seeing the spartan maid's room, I'd expected the owners to be stern-looking, penny-pinching. Instead, Miguel's effusive-ness, the kind where nothing is just fine, but everything is beautiful, every pleasure infinite, reminded me sharply of Papi. As did his courtly gesture as he opened the door for us and ushered us into his house. I remembered Papi's bewil-derment back home when such an act of courtliness on his part was interpreted as chauvinistic. I had returned to another generation as well as another land. It made me see Papi in a new light. How stifling it must have been to always have to tone down his effusiveness, his chivalry, his lifestyle, his tastes.

Mom and the landlady, Graciela, had finished whisper-ing. Graciela nodded and looked at us, "Of course, come in, come in." We soon discovered that Mom had asked if we could visit the altar Graciela and Miguel had set up for the Day of the Dead.

The irony didn't escape me: our father, the non-Canadian, had been the one intent on showing us the real Canada during our cross-country trips, now it seemed it was our mother, the non-Mexican, who was bent on showing us the real Mexico. In this case, the real Mexico's fascination with death. Papi quoted Octavio Paz to me once, and I remembered it still because, at the time, it seemed such a strange thing for a father to say: "by refusing to contemplate death, we cut ourselves off from life." Now I wondered if there was a country somewhere in the world that contemplated people disappearing instead of dying and built altars in their name.

The first thing I noticed was the full baby bottle and soother nestled in between sugar skulls and skeleton figures surrounded by flickering candles and burning copal incense on the top tier of three what looked like orange crates covered in purple crepe paper. My sandals slid, then caught, on ashes and marigold petals scattered at my feet.

"Careful," said Graciela. "The ashes are to show up his footprints when he comes." She took a framed picture of a little boy, a toddler, from the place of honour on the altar and held it out to us. "He was our son," she said.

Faith's stomach chose that moment to rebel. She mumbled something about the incense and motioned for me to help her beat a quick retreat to Mom's home.

Once back in the apartment, Faith headed straight for the bathroom. Mom, who had followed us out, headed for the juicer – "I should have offered you something to drink to begin with. You must be dying of thirst" – and reached for three glasses as she explained that the oranges came from the tree poolside, and that there were bananas too and mangoes, such a luxury to have a private source of fruit outside the front door. I grabbed a glass just as it was about to fall, motioned for Mom to concentrate on the juice, and took down the last two glasses from the open shelf. Her voice blended with the whirring of juicer blades. I scooped emptied orange shells from the sink, dropped them into the garbage can, and let her words wash over me in waves of sound, remembering how I only learned what silence was after Mom left Montreal. Where had Papi's voice fit in, an occasional swell or the tide washing out?

Faith came back finally and dropped into a chair. Mom kept talking with only the briefest glance in her direction. "There you are, Faith, I was just telling Hope about all the fruit we have growing right in the garden here, but even homegrown you can't be too careful, it all has to be washed in purified water and soap, scrubbed with a brush, or else diarrhea strikes. Remember how you always used to call it 'dire rear,' Hope? Or was it you, Faith? Oh well, it doesn't really matter, does it? We got a lot of laughs out of that. Speaking of the Aztec two-step – that's what they call it here – you don't look too well, Faith, a little peaked? Nothing wrong I hope, you always have had the stronger constitution, not like Hope what with her heart murmur…"

I broke in, "Innocent, Mom, an innocent heart murmur." The words brought back the anxious wait nine years ago in the cardiologist's, Mom holding my hand. A murmur no doctor had mentioned before. Maybe it had been shocked into existence. In any case, the cardiologist pronounced it innocent, but it was a verdict Mom never believed.

It was as though I hadn't said a word.

"Now it wouldn't surprise me in the least to see you get sick, Hope, your defences must be so weakened from all those paints, the turpentine, the charcoal dust you work with all the time, you really should be careful. You must install a fan in your studio, I'm sure no one has thought to do that for you and you know how harmful toxic fumes can be and who knows about the added risk just from breathing the air in Mexico City, really I wish you'd asked them to send you here instead…"

Faith broke in before the next wave could gather any strength. "No, there's nothing wrong, Mother." It didn't look like Mom caught the sarcasm. I certainly did. "Other than the fact that I'm pregnant, that is."

Mom and the blender stopped together. A neighbour's rooster crowed outside. And I was the one who was broadsided.

Mom's exclamations, her questions, were only so much background to my whirling thoughts. I went back for the bottle of Tequila I'd noticed on the top shelf and added a shot to my orange juice. I could see the coming months so clearly. Marc, who had always been there for my sister, would of course drop everything and rush to her side. She would have the family I had not, the family I had hoped to rediscover by embarking on the search to find Papi. And I would have José or another man and our tentative attempts at closeness until sex was not enough and he dumped me or I dumped him. Did I want to do it all over again?

Growing up, every single friend I ever had liked Faith best. Quite the testament to friendship if you asked me. The power of those two extra years she had on us spurred my friends to look for inclusion into her world. As if Faith needed them. Did she ever suck her thumb for company or drag an old blanket around until nothing was left but a pocket-sized shred? No. Because she had no need for things or people.

First at everything, me last. Not that I wanted a baby, not now. But still. It made me sick. I added another shot. Not that anyone was going to give a damn if I threw up.

"I'm going to do this myself," Faith was saying. What had I missed?

Mom didn't like that. "Oh, Faith. I think it's a big mistake to set out to do it all yourself. The kind of mistake I made with your father."

"What do you mean?"

Mom ignored the question, clammed up.

Which was a relief.

VI

The search for Papi, the visit with Mom, everything seemed to have been cut short by Faith's announcement. Even the trip Mom had so been looking forward to.

All three of us did leave together on the bus to Xihuatanejo – the land of women, Faith informed us, her Nahuatl lessons already starting to bear fruit – as planned, although Mom didn't hesitate to voice her qualms given Faith's impending motherhood. The beach house that belonged to friends of hers was liveable, however, even if only just, but it soon became obvious Faith would not be able to stay there long. On the one short day our visit lasted she spent most of her time inside, close to the washroom or, the one time she did come with us to the beach, lying on a towel covered from head to toe with a second towel to block the sun out. A stranger walking by could have taken her for a beached whale – a baby whale – covered with a tarp.

On the other hand, the fact that she didn't feel well meant that she never fully realized the extent of her loss. She'd always loved the water: baths, swimming pools, freezing lakes, and seas. Here in the warm waters of this ocean, she would have discovered one more version of the element to love. A version even I loved. I thought of her as I submerged, the waves against my eardrums, and how her musician's ear would appreciate the thrumming of multiple lifeforms underwater like a percussive line from her favourite rock band.

My glimpses of the ocean had been brief before: the Pacific seen from Vancouver, frigid water up to my knees, the ride on the ferry, the cliff past Mile 0 in Victoria on one of the yearly cross-country trips or the Atlantic from our perch on a huge weathered rock close to Peggy's Cove, a country's breadth away. As for Florida – the Quebeckers' promised land – and its shoreline, we'd never been. Papi felt no need to introduce us to the land of the gringos. But in Xihuatanejo, during the short time I had before it was decided for Faith's sake that the two of us should head back, I saw the ocean like never before.

I had only ever seen its surface, from the shore or the shallows or the deck of a ferry, and thought the fascination it exercised came from the waves, the tides, the seagulls, and washed-up shells. But this time, thanks to the snorkel gear – the tubes, masks, and life vests our mother's friends kept in a rattan chest – I was able to see the soul of the ocean and, for me, the never-before-dreamed-of life hidden there: coral reef and brilliant fish instead of surface sameness. Such a shame that a glimpse was all I had.

Mom swam ahead of me, pointing, taking my arm. Every once in a while, she'd hold her thumb up, a sign for me to lift my head out of the water, she had something to say. The resurfacings that I instigated were much more spontaneous, triggered by a mouthful of water I'd let into my tube, or stinging pupils from leaking goggles – a little spit served to solve that.

Each time we broke the surface, I was reminded of the mother killer whale and calf we saw with Papi off the West Coast, the way they crested the waves of the Georgia Strait in unison. So unlike Mom and me – the two of us had none of the killer whales' grace.

Our first concern on resurfacing was to check on our own beached whale on the sand, me still sputtering, dog-paddling furiously, Mom shading her eyes with one hand to see and having to make frantic figure eights with her other hand to keep afloat. Of course, the killer whales' grace was born of long practice. A baby whale had to be taught from the minute it was born when and how to surface since that was where it took each breath. The pair's breathing would be synchronized for as long as mother and calf were both alive. Unlike us, they were creatures of the open sea. Anyway, the point of resurfacing wasn't to mull over what a clumsy whale I'd make. There were more interesting happenings to comment on below.

"Did you see the moray eel?" for instance. How could I have missed it? The sheer ugliness of its huge head, bug eyes, gaping jaw, and wrinkled, trunk-like body and the suddenness of its apparition had made me hyperventilate. Not pleasant at any time, especially not with your lips clamped around a tube. On our next resurfacing, Mom said, "Let's dive down to that cave. An old squid usually hangs out there." I hoped the squid would be less frightening than the eel. Schools of fish eddied around us as we breast-stroked downwards, then, too soon, had to make our way back up. "Did you see the way that tiny damselfish charged us to try to scare us off?" I wasn't sure which fish Mom was referring to. There had been so many, swimming alongside, around, toward me. I immediately fell in love with the name though. "Come on, I'll show you." This time we observed from the surface so as not to be seen as a threat. The damselfish was tiny, dwarfed by the bigger, fiercer surgeonfish and parrotfish it insisted on fending off. They veered away every time. I was the one who signalled for us to resurface. I wanted to know why. Mom obliged.

"Most ocean fish don't have nests you know. They just spawn in open water and swim off. But the damselfish build a nest from empty shells they salvage and clean out, then expend all their energy protecting it and the young they've had once they've found a mate. In patrolling their nest, they patrol and protect the reef as well, keeping all invaders away. And all that despite having no defences, other than their fearlessness…"

She was going to say more, but just then Faith sat up, shielding her eyes. When she spied us, she waved insistently with one hand, the other covering her mouth. I ducked underwater for one last look then flutter-kicked back toward shore, leaving the reef and its inhabitants behind. My flippers turned into impediments as I stood up in shallow water. Gravity was exerting its hold.

Mom wanted to return to Mexico City with us, but Faith insisted that no, we'd be all right, what kind of vacation would Mom have in the big city, stay put, relax, take time for yourself.

Instead, she came to see us off at the bus station that same night. I doubted very much she would do much relaxing though. The worry vein in her throat was pumping double-time, undoubtedly sending extra blood to her brain to fuel more doomsday scenarios, the fallout from the latest turn of events. I wished I was back in the ocean again.

We were first in line outside the bus. I led the way as we waved one last time through the window at Mom and chose the first row behind the driver for the view. I stepped back to let Faith sit down first, but "No, I want to be on the aisle just in case." We'd only just got settled when a woman and her child climbed on board, stopped next to us, and held out their tickets. We were in their seats. I didn't realize seats were assigned. Apologizing, wrestling down my knapsack and Faith's suitcase, jockeying past the woman and child whose seats we'd taken, we moved back eight rows. The whole time unaware how carefully we were being watched, until the trip was over that is, and a kind man gestured for me to go ahead down the aisle behind Faith. A kind man who held a hand up to steady our bags as I grabbed them from the overhead rack but then kept poking and prodding during that long walk down the aisle until we stepped off the bus and I looked over for a glimpse of his suitcase, the one that had been jabbing me from behind. But there was no suitcase, just his faded sweatpants tenting straight out in front of him. Oh great, a pervert Latin-style!

Faith slumped into a chair as soon as we got inside the station. I hoped being two days early wouldn't change José's offer of a ride. I didn't want to have to tackle the metro, not the way Faith was feeling. Especially this late at night. Because of dickpants. He obviously seemed to think we made a perfect target: clueless, gringoesque, and physically weak. He followed me, from a distance this time, as I made my way to the payphones, then over to the magazine stand for change, then back to the phones. I did pass a policía but remembered just in time that Mexico's underpaid cops are often on the make. I couldn't count on any hope of rescue from that quarter. Thank God José was home, which meant it wouldn't be long before we'd be home, too. Although I'd hated to say goodbye to the ocean, I was happy to know I'd be sleeping in my own bed, even shared as it would be, after the last two nights' lack of sleep.

That first night at Mom's place, the church bells started ringing at 3:30 a.m. and kept ringing every half hour. I heard every single chime. They didn't stop until 6. When we finally got up around 10, Mom told us the bells were meant to call the people to 6 o'clock mass. "Originally, I thought we'd go along for the procession to the cemetery to see the picnics and altars set up there, but our trip is going to be tiring enough. Especially now…" Now with Faith's condition. And the second night, when crowds made their way to the cemeteries to be there to greet their departed loved ones, the clanging of bells woke us again at midnight, the same church bells this time summoning the spirits to rise from their graves. I wished we could at least have spent one night in the house by the ocean with only the lapping of waves to disturb our sleep.

Relief was the overriding sensation when José pulled up to the station. He gave me a bear hug then helped me support Faith back into the car. As we sped home, I didn't even close my eyes.

Back in the foul atmosphere of Mexico City, Faith seemed to revive, her nausea kept in check somehow by the thick clouds of pollution that blanketed the sprawling city. Her recovery made sense though, because from the bits of information she let drop, she was long past the first trimester and its morning sickness spells. Into her third trimester actually. Maybe the whole weekend had just been an unfortunate blip on her road to motherhood.

Another unfortunate blip was that the weekend had not given me the hoped-for opportunity to start the wheels in motion by bringing up the subject of looking for Papi. And José burst my one and only bubble when I tried to tell him about snorkelling.

"Why do you keep calling the fish a she?"

I narrowed my eyes, what did he mean?

"It's usually the male damselfish that guard the eggs. That's how they got their nickname: doting fathers." Seeing my disappointed look, José added, "Sometimes both sexes are involved. But never just the female." I wasn't impressed. José laughed, "But then again, fishes can change sex under threat. So I guess it doesn't really matter. Male one day, female the next!"

José refused to talk about his weekend and now he'd managed to put a damper on the only good part of mine. I sighed.

Faith hit the books with her tutor as though the pregnancy would make no difference to her work. I returned to the studio.

I sat in front of my homemade easel, staring. Finally, I placed my hands on either side of the easel bench, swung my feet up in between and, like a gymnast mounting the balance beam, rose to my feet. From this vantage point, I looked down on my figure drawing. Damn. The perspective was off.

Back in Montreal, I used to climb up on a kitchen chair to get a proper bird's-eye view of my work. At school I usually remembered not to, except once in the middle of art class I was so excited about what was taking shape on the sheet of paper that I stood up on my chair without thinking. One of those grade-school desks with the chair attached. My picture looked even better from that angle until I heard the silence. All round. I looked up and saw everyone's eyes on me. The silence was broken by a snicker. A taste of what twenty-six thirteen-year-old boys and girls would have in store for me. I had a choice. Become a target right then and there or act as though I'd been looking for the attention all along.

The choice was easy. I jumped down, grabbed my sketchpad, dropped it on the floor, straightened it out then hopped back on the seat. "Perfect!" I said. Everyone laughed. Not snickered, laughed. Except the teacher, who gave me a DT for disturbing the class. DT. Disturb. Détente.

I lowered myself to a sitting position, thankful for the backrest. The first day José heard me complain about my backaches from standing for hours in the studio or bending over my board at home was the day he built me my special bench.

"No más quejas. I'll build you an easel like you've never seen before."

And he did. I was constantly amazed by the way creativity translated for José into resourcefulness. Twig pencils for the market children, wire twisted into human forms to make bobbing Judas puppets, or clay pots spun on an old potter's wheel to make piñatas he then gave to the children. They

decorated them with papier maché made of recycled spread-
sheets, fringed crepe paper, and homemade glue. The children liked making the piñatas best because of the bulk
caramelos, nuts, and fruit José gave them to stuff inside. As
many sweets ended up in their pockets as in the pots. After
each clay pot – each cántaro – came into being under José's
hands on the wheel, he took it off to mould the extra clay
into seven spikes all around the pot for the children to attach
the streamers to. Although we had always had piñatas for our
birthdays, I'd never realized they stood for anything at all, let
alone Satan and the seven deadly sins. Or that blind faith was
the blindfolded child waving a stick at the piñata. I'd just
thought it was all about free candy.

Now José had made me my very own workbench, my
hobbyhorse we called it. He fashioned a carpenter's bench,
but with a back I could lean into and a horse's crest in front
against which I propped up my board. But even then I
couldn't get my perspective right.

"The best part," José said on the day he presented it to
me, "is this. You straddle the horse like so," he suited the
action to his words, "for a little extra pleasure, stimulation, as
you work." He rocked back and forth, let his eyes close,
began to moan. I laughed. He pulled me down facing him.

"Of course, this is a woman's hobbyhorse, not a man's.
My pleasure doesn't come so easily from a piece of wood."
He grabbed me, drew me close. I felt the bench between my
thighs and José's cock against my belly as he murmured, 'And
he saw that it was good' and laughed.

And I saw that my work was not good. I reached to the
upper left-hand corner of the sheet, made a small tear then
watched its slow descent from there, not guided by my hand,
but by grains of pulp, or maybe gravity's pull. Clouds of charcoal dust, steel grey and rust, puffed out along the line jag-
ging down the model's face – Faith's face actually, since she'd
become my main model – bisecting her Annie bone, then

angling off the sheet. I learned about the Annie bone when I was fourteen, long before I had art classes in musculoskeletal structure. CPR. Cardiopulmonary resuscitation. A way to bring the missing and the dead back to life.

The Annie bone is the inverted V centred in the thorax, the V that a lifesaver must find for rescue to begin. Measure three thumb lengths down to begin pumping so nothing but ribs will crack, not the sharp V that can pierce a lung, or is it the heart? Annie, a lifesize dummy, named after a fourteen-year-old daughter who drowned.

I let the two torn halves slip to the floor.

"I swear I'm suffering from total creative block. I can't draw to save my life. I don't know what's happening." It felt like I was waiting for permission to draw, to paint. Michelangelo didn't ask for permission. I wasn't like Michelangelo, I was more like the boy in that joke gift Faith gave me for my birthday last year along with my hug. The gift I had on my bedside table. The imaginary boy was inside a small plastic box made to look like a shipping crate that fit in the palm of my hand. There were miniature stickers – blue, white, yellow, red, and black, some with pictorals of an umbrella (keep out of rain), a wine glass (fragile), the universal X, an airplane, a hook – pasted to all four sides: DO NOT DROP! HOLD FOR PICK-UP. HANDLE WITH CARE. AIR FREIGHT. DO NOT USE HOOKS! KEEP DRY. DO NOT STACK! PACKING LIST. And what looked like a sticker of an eye in the upper left-hand corner – the eye of the boy. A small button in the upper right-hand corner activated the crate, which began to shake. A pounding sounded at first then a tinny, little voice. "Excuse me, excuse me, excuse me, can you let me out of here?" The voice started out politely enough then built into one long shrill panic-stricken note. Let me out of here. That was me looking for someone, anyone, to give me permission. My art wasn't encased in marble waiting to be found, like Michelangelo's sculptures, rather my artist was imprisoned in a box, one eye glued to the only crack, desperate for a glimpse of the big world outside.

José didn't look like he was really listening to me, he was too busy cutting my fingernails, the nails on my left hand, a skill I didn't have. The one side of my brain dominated so completely that I couldn't even wield a pair of scissors with my right.

José had started dropping around regularly. As though he had found with us what he hadn't found on his trip home. As though the trip to Cuernavaca, his meeting Mom, our unmentioned conspiracy to hide Faith's spell of sickness, had given him special status. Well, maybe that was the wrong word, but somehow we'd skipped past the awkward preambles and were comfortable with the everyday. Like cutting nails.

You'd think nail-cutting would be something a sister could ask her sibling to do. Not me. Faith rolled her eyes the one and only time I asked. She said, "Don't you know nails are meant to be filed? No wonder your hands look like such a mess. All the pigments and solvents aren't any help, either. Have you ever considered moisturizing?"

I hated filing, moisturizing, tweezing, primping. All that bodily housekeeping was too tedious for me. It was only grudgingly that I agreed to do the bare minimum.

With José, I didn't even have to ask. He offered. It felt strange at first, almost like a riff on lovemaking. The strangeness soon wore off. Then it just felt right.

José didn't care whether nails were filed or cut or bitten to the quick. But he did have qualms about removing huge chunks of skin. So he glared at me. Not a real glare. We hadn't crossed that threshold yet.

"Tranquílazate. This isn't easy, you know." It wasn't, either. He was pulling my arm right out of its socket trying to get my hand at the proper angle. I could feel a crick developing in my neck but didn't dare complain. "About your dry spell. You can't draw until you understand. That's what one of my instructors said way back when."

"Ouch!"

"Didn't I tell you to hold still?"

"You've cut too far. My nail will be ingrown. My finger will have to be amputated and then how will I paint!"

"Now that's gringo talk!"

Faith stuck her head around the door. "What's all the noise about? I'm trying to have a nap."

"José was just going to tell me what's so gringoesque about wanting to keep my body parts."

"This should be good."

Faith walked over to the stove, put on the kettle, then sat down at the table where José was bent over my hand again; the torture wasn't over yet.

"Okay, José…"

José raised an eyebrow, dropped my hand to his lap without letting go, and leaned back in his chair. "Don't tell me you've never heard of Frida?"

"Yeahh…?" I said.

"Her art may look surrealistic. It's not. It's fact."

"I haven't heard of her," Faith said.

I answered. "Frida Kahlo. An artist whose life was a living hell. Pelvis impaled with a steel rod because of a bus accident when she was a teen, dozens of operations to try to fix her back and pelvis, leg amputated because of gangrene…"

"Not to mention the abortions and miscarriages, three in all. She couldn't carry a baby to term. She used to keep a foetus in formaldehyde by her bed," José chipped in, only remembering he was speaking to a pregnant woman when Faith recoiled.

I got us back on track. "So you're saying I should have my finger amputated for the sake of my art."

"That's right." He brandished the nail scissors, the kettle screamed, and Faith got up to make her tea.

She should have been at the waddling stage, since she was in her third trimester. She wasn't, but there was a slight something about the way she held herself as she walked. Despite my good intentions, the jealousy I felt was physical. As physical as the scissors grazing my skin. But really, why?

Because I was twenty-four years old? By the time Mom was twenty-four she had had two kids. Whereas me – I sometimes wondered if I'd even grown up yet. Maybe I was a case of arrested development. The arresting officer being my father. My father absconded with my adulthood. He stopped it in its tracks when he left without a word, and carried it into the unknown with him, leaving me with only half a picture of what it was to be grown up. Sounded bizarre enough to be true.

But all teens leave the child's adoring mother/father-love behind. That was part of growing up. Look at José. Even if he had regrets. Maybe that was my problem, I'd never mourned outgrowing my father love, in fact I'd never let myself outgrow him because I always expected him to come back. Could that be it?

Enough navel-gazing already. "Sorry we cut in on your naptime."

Faith sighed. "I can't seem to sleep anyway. I'm all tense. Maybe a bath will do the trick."

José said, "Let me try something first. Here, sit in Hope's chair." I got up and watched as Faith, somewhat reluctantly, switched spots with me. "Now hold out your left hand, palm up. Let me see. Uh-huh, look, there are knots here, here, and here," he stopped talking to point out each trouble spot, "they're blocking the free flow of energy through the body. You just need to get rid of the knots. It might hurt a bit at first." Slowly he began kneading her hand with his thumbs. I watched as the lines around Faith's eyes bunched up with the first pressure, then slowly relaxed. No one said anything for a while. "Now let's try with the right."

When Faith's shoulders dropped an inch, José started talking again. "How's the tub working anyway?"

The tub had been one of Faith's ideas. Like the rental car. José told us after that no one rented cars in Mexico, the cost was too astronomical, a taxi and driver were cheaper no matter how much you travelled. Anyway, we had no bathtub, not in our low-rent hole, but Faith couldn't stand to shower. So one day, she talked José and me into driving to the dump with her in an old pickup truck José borrowed. José tried to tell her that dumps in Mexico weren't like those in Canada and that nothing as useable as an old tub would be found there, the pepenadores would already have resold it, but Faith wouldn't listen.

Not even the stench bothered her. Faith had always had a special gift. She could shut her sense of smell off the same way other people could wiggle their ears. I always thought she must have highly developed muscles or extra flaps inside her nostrils that allowed her to keep odours out. I had no such luck. I had to pinch my nostrils with one hand as soon as I stepped out of the car. Luckily, her faculty of sight was operational and, standing by the car, she needed only a quick scan of the smoking horizon of rubbish heaps to be finally convinced this was not the right place.

We weren't alone. Dirty men and women – pepenadores – off in the distance turned to stare in our direction, their eyes unwelcoming. A group of children made their silent way toward us, staring at the Beetle like they'd never seen a car. José walked over to talk to them, touched a shoulder, an elbow, then walked back to us, his head down. Two men had started walking in our direction, one with a large stick in his hands. Faith said, "I think maybe you're right. We won't find what we're looking for here." All three of us got back into the car, José threw it into first then second, grinding the gears; he hadn't even noticed the advancing men. His thoughts were still with the kids. "It never ends," he said. I wouldn't have been surprised to hear him announce then and there that he'd decided to move the school from the market to the dump. For purely selfish and olfactory reasons, I hoped not.

Faith eventually found what she wanted at Tepito, the huge market José drove us to. It was almost as scary as the dump, lots of beggars, thieves, and even police fencing stolen goods. I wondered whether the claw-footed bathtub we chose was the product of some heist.

Since Ms. Expectant Mother couldn't actually carry the damn thing and risk her baby's life, José and I got to lug it to his friend's truck then up the stairs once we got back, since the elevator was too small. My back muscles would never be the same again. The tub now presided over our bathroom, plunked under the open showerhead that served me quite well.

But Faith wasn't the only one to like the tub. The cockroaches liked it better than the shower, too. Which reminded me of her latest journal entry — it wasn't as though reading it had helped to get her to open up, but I kept going back to it anyway — *Newfound appreciation for cockroaches after two scorpions blew in through the door while at Mom's place. The only good thing was the next gust of wind blew them out again. I'll take cockroaches over scorpions any day. Cockroaches: 3500 species, living fossils, shed exoskeleton several times a year. Females may mate only once, then stay pregnant for rest of life (Christ!), speed on ground, 3 miles per hour. Can squeeze through openings as slim as a dime. Live for weeks without a head. Body count to date: 202.* I still couldn't believe she'd kept count.

José finished kneading Faith's fingers and placed the palms of her hands together as he said, "There you go." Faith actually smiled.

"You," José pointed at me, "You're not finished, remember?"

After another short bout of musical chairs, I turned the conversation back to unfinished business. "Now that you've established that fear of pain is a gringo trait, what would your art teacher have me understand?"

"I don't know. Maybe you need to get to know your subjects better. Establish why you choose them."

I spoke at the same time Faith did. "Like Faith?" "Me?"

He shrugged. "Who knows? Maybe my prof was wrong."

I wasn't so sure about that. Why had I talked Faith into posing? What was it that the new relationship created that I liked? A space where silence made sense? Well, silence of a sort, broken only by the endless tapes of Faith's favourite heavy rock musicians.

José hadn't noticed I'd been sidetracked. He was still talking, "Okay, forget about getting to know your subject better. Maybe boredom's setting in. Why not try a new technique? Beeswax, for instance." He straightened up for a better look, then hunched back over my fingers.

I thought on that one a bit. He just might have hit on a solution. I needed another challenge. It wasn't that I didn't like charcoal and pastel, but I'd decided to try dropping them and the oils because of Mom's constantly expressed concern about carcinogens in the fumes or the sprays I used as fixatives. (Faith and I just rolled our eyes now every time the phone rang since it was usually Mom looking for updates on Faith's condition and my health and filling us in on Cuernavaca happenings. We kept a running record on the wall to see whose turn it was to answer). I missed them. Beeswax would be a natural, inoffensive technique. I started calculating and didn't even notice when José dropped my hand, saying "Ya está." I knew we could find an old Bunsen burner and pans for the studio at Tepito. For the beeswax, surely there were dealers. And I'd need special brushes, lots of them, because until I figured out the right temperatures, there would probably be a few meltdowns. I kissed José's hand, the scissor-holding one, "You're a genius," called out to Faith, "I'll run a bath for you" and rushed off.

I had forgotten about the roaches: three of them genuflecting to the drain. That made 205.

VII

Faith was the one who found the beeswax. Well, Faith through Kiko Albán, her Nahuatl tutor. She'd found him through an ad posted on the bulletin board at the library she went to. She met her tutor every other day to do who knew what. Something related to language and codes, obviously; in any case, one day she asked him about beeswax.

Since she was the one with directions to the market Kiko recommended, the one with a beekeeper who sold beeswax and honey at rockbottom prices, I talked her into being my guide. I pointed out what a great opportunity it would be to see a Nahuatl village and pick up some more vocabulary. There were only so many books on grammatical structure anyone, even Faith, could read.

The market was in Tepoztlán, the same village José had mentioned that first time Faith got sick, on our way to Cuernavaca. We found the beekeeper. I had him set aside the wax and two jars of honey for us then reminded Faith of the hike José had recommended just outside town. Above the town more precisely, on the sandstone cliff. That was where we'd find the temple Tepozteco, used in times past for ceremonies devoted to the god of fertility. Nowadays the ruins at the top of the hill were supposed to be part of some kind of new-age pilgrimage.

"Why are you so keen on us going? So you can debunk the myth?" Faith asked. "Or to pray to the old god of fertility. I don't think so. Not in my case at least, I'm already spoken for." She patted her stomach. "I guess you could pray to Tepoztecatl as the god of pulque. If you want some good cactus juice for the day you run out of beer. He is that, too, you know, the god of pulque. I read it in my guidebook."

She ended up coming anyway. Partway up the hill, in the middle of nowhere on the side of the rocky trail, three native women sat on bright blankets on the ground with handmade jewelry laid out in front of them. I saw two simple silver bracelets, sister bracelets, each with a single charm, that I fell in love with. Faith helped me barter, throwing in a word of Nahuatl from time to time. That didn't bring the price down far enough; I thought we could seal the deal on our way back. But Faith's legs started to give out on her – her legs, her back, her belly, I couldn't know for sure – at the foot of the metal ladder that hung from the cliff a quarter of the way up the trail. I hated to have to turn around, but there wasn't much choice. Faith's only thought was to find a place to sit down. We had to pass by the silver bracelets; the women didn't seem to care.

Back in town, Faith found a bench and told me to go wander for a while. Since she was feeling better by the time I got back, I talked her into following me to the most eclectic shack/boutique I'd ever seen: clothes, sandals, pottery in the avant-boutique, then a wooden chair at the back of the store positioned in front of a bright poncho hanging from ceiling to floor. I led her to the chair and motioned to her to have a seat. A camera stood on a tripod across from the chair. That's when I told her about the snake and what a great painting it would make. Plus, she would be seated the whole time, what more could she ask? Faith gave in quickly enough – her weak spell playing in my favour – although she complained the whole time the salesgirl/photographer/snake charmer draped a five-foot-long garishly yellow reptile around her neck. The snapshot took one minute, my rendition thirty. My sketch took forever because of all the to-and-froing I needed to do to weigh the python in my hands, stroke its scales as it quivered, measure Faith's bicep then the snake's circumference (Faith won). She wouldn't let me wrap it around her belly though.

I filled twenty pages in my sketchbook. At one point, Faith said, "Next thing you'll be licking that snake!" She didn't understand how the eyes see only illusion and the other senses are the ones an artist needs – or this artist anyway – to tap into reality. I didn't even know how to begin to tell her.

The biggest revelation for me was Faith's entry the next day. In her journal. Which I'd taken my usual precautions to consult. As though I was hooked or something. Like I needed my fix. We couldn't seem to talk about the things that mattered – Faith's pregnancy, Papi's whereabouts, what we really thought – but at least I could read her written words. After all, José was the one who said I needed to understand.

Asked Kiko the Nahuatl terms for snake, foetus, gringa.

Taught him English word Gitchiegoomeism. The habit of placing natives outside history. Asked him if Nahuatl is like Cree, distinguishing between what is animate (nature but a pencil too because it brings paper to life) and what is not (every part of the human body except the spirit and the heart).

He told me a new Spanish word: pintura negativa. Technique using beeswax and paintbrush. No more paintings of empty chairs and lonely clothes in a closet for Hope. All these years, she has never clued into the fact that they were her way of translating Papi's absence. Now she can spend her time translating that absence with every negative stroke of her brush.

Pintura negativa. I didn't even know the technique had a name. She was right. I'd often gazed at my paintings for long stretches of time, watching for movement from the corner of my eye, straining to sense how long the chair, the room had been vacated, or when the unseen presence would return. It came to me that I'd never considered what Faith might be thinking when she modelled for me. I wondered what else she'd found out about me during those times, things I hadn't figured out for myself.

I flipped through my sketchbook. Without meaning to or wanting to, I'd worked the market snake down over Faith's collarbone, under her breast into a demi-lune cradling her swollen gut, her protruding ribs. Just what she hadn't wanted. Then I looked again. Protruding ribs. They registered for the first time. Why would a pregnant woman lose weight?

The next evening, Faith had Nahuatl-related plans with Kiko, and I slept over at José's apartment.

Sleeping over had always felt more real to me than the sex act. No one could sustain the sexual performer in them through an entire night. A person sleeping beside me was no longer acting; a character didn't look out from eyes that opened to the first morning light. Instead the eyes said *this is me and nobody else.*

It started out as just a dinner. I had to turn down his invitation at first because my clothes situation had gotten desperate. I was going to have to find a laundromat. "Laundromats are for gringos," he said. "Just take it to a washerwoman." I tried to explain I couldn't wait the time that would take. "Okay, I'll go with you then," he said. "And then we'll go back to my place for dinner." Romantic as all get-out. Actually, to me a joint outing to the laundromat did seem a bit too intimate at first. But I was sick of washing all my clothes by hand.

After our day with the market kids, we went our separate ways to pick up our clothes. José suggested I grab a snack to tide me over.

I couldn't believe how much dirty laundry I had. I'd been washing my underwear and a few of my other standards once a week. For the rest, I'd been able to hold off by rotating clothes. My paint-stained T-shirts and shorts could just stay that way. I didn't even bother bringing them home, instead I left them at the studio and spritzed them with patchouli oil from time to time to rid them of the smell of paint and turpentine and sweat.

The laundromat José knew of was in my direction so we decided he would stop by for me. By the time I went through the closet and my trunk, I had a black garbage bag full of clothes. I tried hoisting it up on my shoulder only to think that maybe handwashing in the sink wasn't such a bad idea after all.

I left the bag in the bedroom to answer the door. José wasn't carrying a thing. At my look of surprise, he kissed me then turned and pointed over his shoulder at the knapsack on his back. Then he asked, "Where's yours?"

I ducked into the bedroom and came back dragging the garbage bag across the floor.

José whistled. "If I'd known, I would have suggested this two weeks ago!"

He shrugged one shoulder out of the knapsack and swung it around and off. "I've got some room left. Let's share the load." He motioned for me to open the bag.

I held back for a minute, but José didn't notice because he was undoing the drawstring at the top of his pack. Funny how this could seem more revealing than making love.

He crouched, waiting by his open bag. At least he wasn't going to take my panties out himself. I kept my head down as I grabbed two handfuls of dirty clothes and stuffed them inside. I didn't watch as he pulled the drawstring tight.

The garbage bag was easier to carry now. I held it with both hands over my shoulder.

The ten machines were all spinning so we went back outside on the steps to wait. A stray dog lay in the shade against the wall. The fur on its flank was all matted except for two bare patches that still showed the mark of another dog's teeth.

Dogs scared me back home, but not here. Dogs in Montreal were unpredictable, always barking and growling and ready to lunge. Dogs here just seemed to cower.

On the street in front of the laundromat there was a tope, kind of like the speed bumps at home to slow cars down only this one was much bigger and came to a point along the top. Most cars seemed to consider it more like a ski jump. We could hear engines revving before the cars hit, then watch them sail through the air a couple of feet. The dog didn't stir as each car landed with a thud; its ears didn't even twitch.

The door to the laundromat was wide open. We could hear the click of a machine going off then the spin cycle slowing. José stood up and held out his hand for me.

The only other people inside were a couple in their forties. He was big and burly, looking like he'd come straight from his job as a butcher, all dressed in white with red and yellow stains. He sat while his wife/companion did all the work. He watched as she gathered all the laundry up in her arms and walked it over to the dryers at the back. I had started to empty my bag into the bin when José said, "You're sure you don't have any colours that will run?"

"I don't think so," I hoped I was right. "Oh no, I forgot to bring change for soap."

"Don't worry, I've got some right here," and José unzipped the front pocket of his pack.

He pulled up a chair for me. It was orange plastic with holes and shaped like a bowl. "When the clothes are done, we can use the chairs as laundry baskets."

The other man made a show of patting his shirt pockets with both hands looking for cigarettes then stood up and shook his head as he walked out, "First time I hear a man tell a woman how laundry should be done. Qué mundo!" I got the giggles and couldn't stop.

Dinner was another treat: marinated chicken, frijoles, rice, and tortillas. José showed me how to heat the tortillas up as needed on a grill set on his two-burner hot plate – José didn't have the luxury of a separate room for the kitchen – then he transferred them to a covered basket. I was glad the sight of sweating men pushing their trolleys full of plucked yellowing carcasses on the streets leading to the market hadn't made me go back on my decision to keep chicken on the list of non-mammals I would eat. José had a secret marinade that made even tough chickens tender.

José rolled his tortilla into a sausage shape to push the rice and frijoles onto his fork. On every second bite, he reached into a jar by his plate, pulled out a jalapeño, and popped it into his mouth. Sweat pearled at his hairline and trickled down his forehead, his nose, and his cheeks. He offered me the jar. I had heard that hot peppers were great for killing parasites so I took one jalapeño just in case, placed it between my lips for a bite then threw it onto the table as both my mouth and tongue caught fire. I took a swig of Dos Equis while José laughed at the expression on my face.

His wasn't a show of machismo. He just loved the extra picante the jalapeño brings. If he were a true macho, he wouldn't heat tortillas or do laundry, he'd strut like my peacocky studio owner or refuse to play kids' games. He'd rule me out as a lover because of my cut-off shorts or peasant skirts and paint-stained T-shirts with rolled-up sleeves and

Birkenstocks – natural birth control Marc used to call them –
a far cry from the form-hugging dresses and high heels or
iron-creased jeans and starched snappy white blouses most
women in Mexico wore. My body type was more like a
Mexican woman's though; Mexican men didn't seem as fix-
ated on breasts as their North American counterparts were.

We made love after dinner, fueled by jalapeños and beer.
I'd already seen how far from macho José was in bed. He
didn't dismiss foreplay as an incidental, a prior-thought,
unimportant in the grand ejaculatory scheme. He knew the
importance of a woman's pleasure whenever it came.

Afterwards, I was ready to lie there forever. Instead José
said, "Bueno," and I said, "Don't say that."

"What do you mean? What's wrong with 'bueno'?" he
half-laughed.

I pulled him closer, "When you say 'bueno,' it doesn't
mean 'good,' it means 'so then, that's over, what should we do
next?' We don't need to do anything next. This is good."

José pulled me up to a sitting position. "No, you're
wrong. Trust me. Let's get dressed."

It was shortly before midnight when we left his apartment. José linked his arm with mine, while a net bag swung
from his free hand.

The streets weren't empty the way they'd be back home.
There were groups of people strolling, children running in
circles, music pouring out from the open doors of restaurants
and bars. The streets were dark with very few streetlamps so
I was taken by surprise when a young boy stepped in front
of us, brandishing the chicles he had for sale. I fished for
change in my wallet and he asked, pointing at the billfold, "Is
that where you keep the other money?" His question sounded
so wistful, it was as though he was talking about a forbidden
land. I snapped the change purse shut, pulled a paper bill
from the side pocket and watched him start, stare, then run
off waving it at his friends.

Finally, the dark narrow street we'd been following led out onto the huge expanse of the Zócalo. The tents of activists already protesting the coming implementation of the free trade agreement – the TLC again – dotted the main square, more visible now than during the day, glowing eerily from the Coleman lights or candles inside as the campers got ready for bed.

"We have to come back here around Christmastime," José said. "It's really something to see." We sat down on the sidewalk with our feet sticking into the road – the authorities must have thought benches would encourage loitering; a lot of good their forethought did – and José opened the net bag, bringing out a coconut. "I bet," José said, "that this will be a first." He gestured toward the lopsided cathedral across the square as he raised the coconut high and brought it smashing down against the sidewalk's edge. Just then the first bell pealed. The coconut's dark outer husk of fibres split in two, showing bright coconut flesh shining under the watery milk. I let the juice trickle down my throat as I counted the strokes – two, three, four – all the way to twelve. When I looked down again, José was holding out his penknife, a chunk of coconut speared on the tip. I took it in my teeth, gingerly, aware of the blade beneath, the flesh crunchy not pulpy, belying its name. I wished it were José's flesh instead. I let go, turned my head, and bit the side of his hand. He let the pocketknife drop.

I wanted one of those squatter's tents right then and there to use as our love nest. The nest of a damselfish, an empty coconut husk. We hurried back to the apartment instead, made love on his single bed, then fell asleep, front to back, José's hand on my breast, his leg between my thighs.

VIII

Faith actually hissed at me. "I can't believe you talked me into this."

"What?" I looked around. Anouk, the Swiss artist, was just leaving. I could hear her calling out to Alan and Claude to wait up. I would have liked to tag along. Another day.

"What do you mean? I thought everything went great." Faith had agreed to model for our studio group's Monday morning session. I introduced her to Anouk, Alan, and Claude, and we all did a good morning's worth of work. I made sure we didn't tire Faith out: for most of the poses we had her do she was either sitting or reclining. I even lugged her boom box to the studio along with some of Faith's favourite tapes to play in the background: Luba, Melissa Etheridge, Jeff Healy, Bryan Adams.

I sometimes played a game with myself, wondering what other people would paint if they could. But it didn't work with Faith because her pictures would be made of notes played on an electric guitar.

The others had visibly chafed over her long warm-up. Most models did a few jumping jacks and twists to get their circulation going and their bodies limber before the modelling session. Faith did Hatha Yoga. She said she couldn't model until she'd balanced the right and left sides of her body and brain.

Discipline was the key to yoga. It was only natural that yoga should find Faith. Actually, Papi gave her yoga. Before he grew beyond it, as he said, to concentrate on meditation. As I watched Faith do her ten sun salutations, holding every asana with perfect form, I could hear Papi's voice calling off the sequence. Remember him telling me how meditation was an acknowledgement of pain without actually being the pain. I hadn't understood what he meant. Papi had been in one of his hyper phases. The meditation at least served to calm him down.

"You didn't even have a bloody screen up for me to get undressed behind. Do you know how embarrassing it is to undress in front of complete strangers?"

"But, Faith, you've just spent three hours modelling nude for total strangers. What does it matter that…?"

"Not just any strangers, strange men! You didn't tell me there'd be men here, too."

"Faith, they're artists. You were their model."

"I felt like I was doing a striptease. I kept expecting them to throw money at me or something. No one even had the decency to look away."

I wanted to explain to her that if Alan, Claude, or Anouk didn't look away, it wasn't out of voyeurism. They would have seen the folds her shift sank into as she dropped it on the floor, the slow gentle release of her breasts from her bra, the way the line running from the top of her head down her arm paralleled the line of hip to leg as she bent over to step out of her panties. I thought better of it though, realizing Faith would not be comforted to hear she'd been seen not as a person but as a thing in motion, a form, a shape. Whoa, could that be my reason for wanting to paint her? That might take some thinking. But Faith wanted an answer right away.

"Caramba, Faith, no one else has ever complained. I'm sorry if it bothered you. Next time…"

"Caramba yourself. There won't be a next time."

I sighed.

Faith jammed the cassette tapes back into their cases and dumped them in the woven bag she'd started using as a purse. The Aztec look, bought on a flea market expedition with Kiko, another exercise in increasing her word power. "You can bring the boom box later on your way home. Incidentally, you should take up yoga. All that sighing is a clear sign you're not getting enough air into your system."

Faith's system was obviously not lacking for air, especially the hot kind. I stuck my tongue out at her as she walked through the doorway. She made me feel like I'd never grow up.

To calm down, I walked around the room, looking at the sketches the others had left behind. The noon sun was streaming through the skylights, and blobs of dropped wax on the floor had started to melt, leaving tiny pools of colour that shone in the light. No one had bothered to put chairs or easels away. I had to weave around Claude's frame and his paint-stained director's canvas chair. The technique he'd come up with was a frame laid flat on two orange crates. He too was sick of standing up. José and I had actually emptied those crates for him a couple of weeks ago; a lot of the oranges I took home, but some José and I ate in the studio together one night after making out. José came up with a new game that night. He'd throw a section up in the air, say "watch this," drop his head back, mouth wide open, and let the orange fall in with a plop. We went through three oranges that way, until I started getting a stomach ache. Not all three oranges ended up in our bellies though, a number of them stuck to the ceiling. Over the next few days, I'd be pulled out of my concentration by an orange section plummeting to the floor. They left behind a faint copper-hued stain.

Claude fancied himself another Picasso. His paintings were an ode to dismemberment, in Faith's case to what looked like a broken neck. It made me wonder sometimes what women had ever done to him. Or why he didn't spend more time looking for the good instead of imagining the bad. Enough said.

Anouk was in her rock phase. Not music-rock, stone-rock. She said rocks were linked to the soul. Her rocks just looked like misshapen potatoes to me. She refused to give them any shape because she said sculpted rock desacralized sacred labour. She said her rocks symbolized freedom, while sculpted rock only symbolized servitude. True to form, she had zeroed in on Faith's belly, and made it look something like a big potato ending in a cone-ish head.

Alan's painting was the one that really interested me. Sometimes I wondered if there was a North American sensitivity. Whether those of us on the North American continent – Canadians, Americans, and Mexicans – didn't have, in spite of all our differences, a common world view. A view that the Old World, the Europeans, couldn't even imagine. We were the New. Not yet ossified. We were from a world where nature and the elements were still a force to contend or bargain with as with gods, not something centuries of industrialization had fought to beat into submission. Alan's drawing felt to me like intuition at work. Looking at it I got the feeling he knew my sister better than I ever would. In the close-up of her features, he had uncovered the grey of vulnerability that translated into the black of outrage.

I'd have to ask José one of these days to tell me what he thought about the others' work. He'd already told me what he thought of mine. One day he popped by early to walk me to the market. He toured the half-finished offerings lined up along my wall. Four artists, four walls – a good thing there weren't any more of us. José struck an art critic pose.

"I note," he said, drawing on an imaginary pipe, "that in every manifestation of her life's work, the artist has avoided placing the action, the figures, and the light in the centre of her canvas. This tendency," he tapped the invisible pipe on the edge of the sink as he walked past, "is a sign of in-betweenitude, off-centredness. Of an artist unbalanced. Además," – here he peered out at me from underneath the imaginary brim of an imaginary hat – "I notice that she the artist is always left of centre, very telling don't you think?"

I laughed. "No, you've got it all wrong. I'm just off to the side, patrolling, wondering how I got here and why. Plus, who are you to be judging my art? You're colour-blind. You told me so yourself."

José waved away my interruption. "As I was saying, this left-of-centredness, could it speak of communist leanings à la Rivera, a wish to overthrow the state? She is either a grand subversive or someone who should wear glasses to see straight."

I would love to hear his criticism of Claude's pseudo-Picassos, Anouk's lumpy bits of rock, and Alan's greys to blacks.

"We also note here," José pointed to the folds of a blanket clutched to the model's chest, "that this artist who specializes in nudes is afraid of the nakedness of the Other. Every example of her obra calls on props – a flower, a blanket, a cushion, partial clothing, a snake – in an attempt to cover up. Very suspect."

"What about your Judases, your piñatas of evil, your artist's easels in the form of masturbation tools? Seems to me they show a man overly preoccupied with sin and punishment."

"My heritage, amor mía," he shrugged. We laughed while *amor mía* kept ringing in my head.

My workplace was a jumble of pots, burners, half-melted wax. With the new technique I was having trouble judging the right temperature or the right amount of pressure to exert, and I ended up discarding most of the canvases I started. I sighed again, then caught myself. Time to clean up and go home.

Faith was well into her third trimester. So why was she still retching, this time behind the bathroom door? She walked out looking yellow, a jaundiced version of herself.

"You've got to go see a doctor," I said for the nth time.

"What for? I'm pregnant. I'm supposed to be sick."

"I don't know, Faith. Not for this long. Not this bad."

"Anyway, I've been. To the American hospital. They ran a few tests."

"And what did the tests say?"

A pause. "You know, not much."

"As far as I can see, you don't need a test to tell you something's wrong. All you need is a pair of eyes."

"And what would you suggest?" she tried to sound offhanded but didn't quite pull it off.

"I don't know. There's got to be someone else. I'll look into it if you want."

Faith shrugged. Unconvincingly. I wanted to grab her and separate her shoulders from those blocked ears. So she'd already been to the hospital. Why hadn't she mentioned it before? From the way she was acting, I suspected she was worried herself. She knew I was in any case. She even wrote it herself: *Hope's worried. Bond between us must be stronger than I thought.*

A bond? Felt more like bondage to me. Worry had that tendency and explained why I couldn't let her be. Worry or guilt, hard to tell which. Maybe that explained why I couldn't let Papi be, either. Why I felt his absence, her illness, like a rough cord wrapped around my body, constricting every movement, chafing my skin, rubbing me raw. If I had only listened or read his words, he might not have left. What had Faith said or written that hadn't clicked?

In the apartment I shared with Faith, there were moments when I was beginning to feel like I was living in a fish tank.

A very specific fish tank: the old one we used to have when we were little. All the fish had died so we converted it into a home for the baby frogs we caught with Papi on Mont-Royal in a ditch not far from Beaver Lake. They were small, no bigger than the end of my thumb, and tan in colour with black markings: two markings that looked like an X in the centre of their back and others up the flanks and ringing their little frog legs. Our mother called them spring peepers, but said it was too early in the breeding season for us to hear their peeps. She told us they breathed through their skin, through their pores. Papi didn't know what they'd be called in Spanish.

One day soon afterwards, Papi came home with a lizard that we put in with the frogs. Faith and I didn't make the connection at first when the number of frogs started to drop. We couldn't figure it out. Not until the day I saw a frog sitting on the lizard's snout. I stuck my face right up against the glass to watch the two friends at play only to realize that the frog's leg was actually inside the lizard's mouth. The frog was being eaten alive, silently and very, very slowly.

It was a lizard-like force that I felt invading our home without warning. Invading Faith. A force neither of us acknowledged, at least not out loud. If only it would take shape, then I could take it on, chase it down. Despite the joys of sleeping over at José's, I felt increasingly obliged to stay at home, just in case. José wasn't too happy, either.

"Hey, what about me?"

"I already told you. It's better for me to stick close to home right now while Faith is feeling this way."

"So for the next couple of months, you'll be tied up holding your sister's hand? That's just great."

His tone made me snap back. "You mean I should be here holding your hand instead?"

José wouldn't give up. "Faith just feels vulnerable right now. She's blowing a normal thing like pregnancy out of proportion. A case of hypochondria. She doesn't need a nursemaid, she needs a therapist." At my furious glare, he said, "Oh, just forget it." And stopped talking.

I tried to convince myself I was angry at José's selfishness, reducing everything to what he wanted. Really though, when I looked at it, he had just given voice to one of the very thoughts I had been trying to keep at bay. If he was right, if Faith's illness was only in her mind, then what did that mean?

José wouldn't be any help to me in exploring for further meaning. He too was angry now, and I discovered he was the kind who did anger by clamming up. Just what I needed. Another person whose feelings I'd have to guess at. I stood up, walked over to the fridge for a beer, and started to walk back.

"Don't you think you've had enough?" he said. I stopped in mid-track.

"What was I thinking? Of course, you're right." I took two steps over to the sink and poured the can's contents out. "Anything else while we're at it? Another family member to cut loose, another teetotaler's meeting to attend, another…" then I burst into tears. I so envy people who can turn anger into a weapon they use to accomplish their ends. Instead of being manipulated by it, letting it turn them into a blubbering fool.

José came up, put his arms around me, and hid his face in the crook of my neck. "I'm sorry. I shouldn't have said anything. It's just… I don't want to see you hurt yourself."

I didn't bother trying to speak. Words never make it past my tears.

Skin against skin woke me up. I opened my eyes to Faith's bulging belly wedged in against me, the mattress flaring up on either side of our two sweating bodies. Damn, I fell asleep on the edge of the bed, not in the middle. Bloody mattress. I punched at the mound rising above me and hauled myself over and away from Faith's clammy skin. She rolled onto her back, still asleep. In that position, I could see why she'd nick-named her belly Mount Vesuvius.

I sat up on my elbow to get a better look at her. It was then that I saw the baby shift. A tiny elbow – or maybe a foot – jabbed out just to the left of Faith's bellybutton. I reached down and stroked the projecting ridge. The baby's movements grew more restless, rippling Faith's belly like an octopus inching through. If only I could touch my niece. I wondered if Faith felt the same way harbouring her baby. How could she share one body, one bloodstream, one life-giving cord with her child, and not touch?

I lay back down and wished for the cord tying me to Faith to cut me some slack. Finally, when it was obvious I wasn't going to get any sleep, I snuck out of the room, grabbed my clipboard and pencil: blunt, 3B, black. Charcoal. Supposedly the most sensitive and responsive of media, a medium becoming more sensitive as the days went by. Tone was differentiated, space modelled, form accentuated by eras-ing the charcoal strokes and shading that were laid down. Figures took shape where only blackness existed.

True form came from the unseen. Never had this been truer: Faith lay there naked, sheets thrown back, the round of her belly hiding the essential from the eye. The unmoving surface concealed a rich undercurrent of action – blood and nourishment coursing through the umbilical cord, thumb to mouth, tiny foot kicking out.

There was the model, then there was the canvas. I couldn't tell yet what traces would be left of the moment I stole from

Faith. When I drew, my mind shut down, but my wrist continued its rotation around the axis of my little finger. It was
then that another form, another force hidden in Faith's belly
leaked from my pencil tip. The form wasn't a baby, but something else. It frightened me. It kept on surfacing.

Which was why I couldn't let Faith see what I created.

IX

I had to figure out what to do about Faith. In the meantime, I had to put in time at the studio. That's what it had become. Putting in time. Beeswax was not a suitable replacement for charcoal, even less so for oils. I hated all the fuss, the wobbly pots, the burner that took eons to heat up, the way the wax hardened within minutes of being removed from the flame, forcing me to work at assembly-line speed.

So beeswax worked three hundred years ago? Maybe some of what we'd seen over the past few centuries had been progress, which I would do well to take note of.

I was starting to think that maybe it was okay that my art wasn't the be-all and the end-all. My father was a good example. The only way I can figure it, his poetry must have been more important to him than us or anything or anyone else in his life. When Papi wrote about his experience, the facts always had to bow to the rhyme. The me I saw inside his poems was not the me outside. Our lives bowed to his poetry until he in turn bowed out of our lives. That was the explanation I'd come up with for his leaving. José said most things have no explanation, they just have to be taken on faith. He'd probably recited the same mantra to himself. José and I were okay again. He had backed off, something I discovered he could do much easier than I could. I worried at things, couldn't leave them alone, was drawn to them in spite of myself. I guess you have to have faith to begin with in order to let things be.

Instead of setting out supplies, I went to the army-green filing cabinet that sat in the corner. It was an abandoned cabinet José and I found behind one of the shattered buildings – still not rebuilt all these years after the earthquake – and brought back here. Mexico, country of extremes, not just of rich and poor, but of nature: earthquakes, eruptions, hurricanes, burning meteorites.

They say the beginning of the end for the dinosaurs began here in what became Mexico, in the Yucatan peninsula, tens of millions of years ago, after a huge volcanic eruption. The ash particles blocked incoming sunlight and the earth cooled. Either that or a giant meteorite fell and started massive fires whose smoke cut off the sun.

Afterwards the only survivors were mammals, spared because their offspring had shelter in the mother's womb from the acid rain that followed. They and egg-burying birds and reptiles. We humans and the ostriches. Survival was more likely with your head in the sand.

I popped my head out of the sand and into the drawer of a filing cabinet that had made its own fifteen-storey plunge during a life-altering earthquake and survived. The top drawer jammed, the empty guide rails were all bent, and my application sat inside.

THE ARTIST AS CONDUIT. What did I used to think an artist was? I flipped past the cover page, the index, the chronological description of my nine enclosed slides and on to page one. "I believe in art ruled by intuition, where the need for translation disappears." Becoming one's subject, nothing in between. "I believe an artist's inner world should dictate her gaze, yet allow for the transcendance of the limits of experience." Faith had helped me fill out the form. As if it didn't show. She made me put a foreword in the essay with all the possible definitions of intuition, saying the meaning wouldn't be clear otherwise.

Maybe I'd reached an impasse because my intuition was telling me something I didn't want to hear and even less see.

I pulled a tube of oil paint from the half-open worktable drawer. Weighing it there in my hand, I felt nostalgic. I remembered the minimal effort involved in using oils. The way the paint oozed out onto my worktable in one spurt, lent itself to infinite combinations of tint and hue, and waited, moist and pliant, for my return. Mountains and valleys of colour laying out their geography. What did my mother know? Why humour her? So she wouldn't have to worry about toxic fumes wending their way up my nostrils, down my throat, and into my lungs? Or, more to the point, so she wouldn't blame me?

I was twenty-four years old. I hadn't lived with my mother for seven years. Whether she worried or not, life kept happening. She couldn't protect us any more than she could protect herself. I was tired of her routine.

Then the idea came. One that had been seeping into my brain from the time José and I first met. Me watching José as he built a blackboard stand for the market school, or created my easel. Together we could make some incredible frames. Layered frames. My main canvas fitted with miniature doors that opened to a canvas behind. The flat oil finish of the visible painting giving way to a secret world beneath, no longer just painted but tactile. Papier-machéd scraps of ripped sketches, bottle caps, marbles, keys, miniature toys glued to curved recessed walls. A painting for touch, not just for eyes.

Despite the heat, I set out at such a pace that I was almost running, attracting wide stares from the other people crowding the street. As I approached, I saw the market kids pointing, laughing at José standing behind Guillermo straddling a park bench, his head leaning on the backrest, José's hands on his skull working in brown suds. Guillermo from Guerrero. Thirteen years old, surviving on his own.

"It's about time," José called out. "You're on delousing duty. How about you bring us some fresh water?"

I walked over and squeezed Guillermo's knee. He seemed to enjoy being the centre of attention. I considered whether this was a good time to ask José for a favour, decided against it, and instead grabbed the faded plastic basin at his feet and made my way over to the old wash house and the rusty pump.

"Now, Guillermo, get up on your knees and lean way over, dóblate, while Esperanza gives us some of that water." Esperanza was José's name for me. A translation of Hope. "Just dump it over his head, that's it." José's hands snaked down through Guillermo's hair, pushing the black foam out and away. God, what kind of soap was it! "Now Benjamin, you go get us some more water, and it'll be your turn next." Benjamin, seven, was already up, grabbing the basin from my hands, the leftover water sloshing up over the rim onto his T-shirt. "Guillermo, you move over to that bench, and Esperanza will check to see we've got them all. You don't mind, Esperanza? There's my comb." José nodded behind him with his chin.

"No funny stuff," he said in English with a smile as I squeezed my hand into his back jean pocket. "There are minors present." Then back to Spanish. "If you find any lice, it's on to Plan B. Off with his hair." He flourished his Philips shaver, a battery-operated gift from me.

It was definitely time to call my life's work into question when digging lice eggs out of tar-encrusted roots seemed like a better way of spending my time than working in the studio. But maybe that was about to change. Meanwhile, I called out quite happily, "I think we're on to Plan B." I wasn't quite as happy when the first lice egg turned up on my own skull. Faith even less so when she heard she needed to be deloused. But by then lice eggs were the least of our worries.

X

Faith's next journal entry was totally devoid of her precious facts.

Test results are in. And gamma rays are out. Snake hold tightening.

El pueblo, unido, jamás será vencido.

Gamma rays? The snake again? A battle cry? Where did Faith write the speed of light? Where was her description of rattles, scales, shedding of skin? When had she ever strayed from the facts? I didn't understand.

I confronted her that night while she took her bath, her Biafran belly breaking through surface foam. Water pooled in her clavicle bones, so pronounced on either side of her throat. I confronted her not with the diary – I wasn't that stupid – but with everything else. "You know, I would really like to feel that I'm your sister and not some university-appointed roommate. Sisters are supposed to talk. They've even been known to confide in each other once in a while. I won't run off, whatever it is, so tell me. Faith, you're almost eight months pregnant, but you look like a scarecrow with a pumpkin sticking out front. This far into a pregnancy, the routine is not for women to throw up occasionally. Their eyes don't wear bags to their knees, and their knees still have the strength it takes to climb up a couple of stairs. What's wrong, Faith? What's happening?"

Faith's eyes shot me a look then she slowly slid down until the water bubbled up over her face and only floating tendrils of hair appeared between the suds.

I left to write the letter. The time had come to act. Once finished I walked down to the lobby of the hotel next door and had the letter faxed to Montreal. I'd done what any sister would.

～

"Tell me you didn't send this!" Pissed-off didn't even begin to describe Faith's tone. She was standing at the foot of the bed, her head encased in a bathtowel turban, my fax in her hands. I should have hidden it, just like my book of quotes.

Faith started reading aloud, "*Dear Marc,... I have two bits of news... you're going to be a dad. You'll make a great dad... But Faith's not just pregnant, she's sick. She needs you...I thought it was about time she filled you in...* You thought!"

My best defence was a counterattack. "What of it? This is something you should have done ages ago."

"You sent it! You actually sent it! Christ. *She needs you?* You sent that, too. When have you ever heard those words cross my lips? When?"

"There's no point getting worked up over nothing. This is Marc we're talking about. Your lover, the father of your baby." I tried to sound reassuring.

Faith wasn't listening. "Who gave you the right...!"

I opened my mouth, but nothing came out. Maybe I had slightly over-interpreted the situation. Faith hadn't mentioned Marc's name since she arrived in Mexico.

"You idiot. You really think Marc needed to hear it from you? He knows I'm pregnant. He heard it from me. Months ago. He doesn't want a baby. I don't want him. We are no longer an item. Period."

"But… you said you didn't…"

"What are you? My confessor? I don't tell you everything. It's none of your business. This is my baby and mine alone."

I had screwed up, even I could see that.

Seeing was not my strong suit. The only way truth made itself known to me was through my other senses and my hands. Maybe I should become a masseuse, learn to know the people around me through their massed muscles, knotted nodules, and cramped calves. Maybe then I'd have a better feel.

I could envision Marc again, lying on our kitchen table in Montreal, naked except for boxer shorts, his chest and arms criss-crossed with red, yellow, and black lines. Faith sat on the window ledge, my art class anatomy book on her lap. I, with felt markers in hand, traced down from Marc's chest to his thighs. I was studying for my anatomy exam, Faith was reciting the muscle groups, and I was tracking them down Marc's body, getting him to flex for emphasis every once in a while. He put up with me like an annoying kid sister, no matter the lack of blood ties. "Maybe Marc should be my end-of-year project," I said, "I can enter him in the student art exhibit." Marc faked a punch at me; Faith said, "He's not abstract enough." Not as abstract as the father who could have been, as opposed to the simple donor of sperm. I pretended not to remember the ridiculous envy I felt at the cozy threesome I thought they would make: Faith, Marc, the baby. What had I missed? I was beginning to think I could paint a whole fresco of the things I had missed or the memories lost to me. The images, words, sounds, and smells that never left a mark. Did they ever exist?

I used to think that anything I forgot couldn't have been central. That in forgetting, I shed the peripheral, the posturing, the contrived. What if I was wrong? What if I, like other artists I knew, should have devoted myself to camera art: taking pictures, carrying snapshots to my loft, painting from the perspective of thousands of sensitized dots instead of from my senses. I used to scoff and pretend that in front of a camera the models mutate, deviate, and lose their intrinsic grace.

That night I sneaked out while Faith was asleep and went to José's. The streets didn't seem as friendly or joyous in the dark on my own. I was glad to reach his door.

As a lover, José was like the best kind of artist, one who knows the one true way to work with a model. When an artist and model first begin working together, especially when they're of the opposite sex, a good artist will be gentle and undemanding. He'll ask only for poses in which the model can protect her most private spaces and parts. As rapport and trust are established, the poses evolve: from a lotus position with a cushion hugged up close to one without cushion or drape. To one where legs come uncrossed, arms are outstretched, and her whole being, both inner and outer is exposed. As a lover, I felt I had never been brought to this point before, and I was grateful, still unbelieving, that it could be so.

Afterwards, in bed together, I listened to his breathing and noticed the way my breath slowed to match his until our two spooning bodies breathed as one. I hated Marc then. How could he reject Faith and his own child? What had my tracing in felt pen not shown up? Then I thought of the baby and Papi. And José and his dad. Maybe losing a father hurt less if you'd never known him to begin with.

XI

I decided to make a peace offering to Faith. A book of poetry. I have to admit that my original reason for being in a bookstore wasn't to find some suitable token of atonement for having tried to contact Marc behind Faith's back. Luckily, the fax had been returned to us, the number no longer in use. Knowing that Faith's baby would be fatherless strengthened my resolve to find a father somewhere. Ours if not hers. And to break with the family tradition that seemed to be in the making. I wanted my niece to have memories she didn't have to fabricate: a real face and a real voice to call up when she needed them.

I'd decided the best place to search for Papi was to comb the bookstores, to look for books of poetry bearing his name. Books with recent dates, a publisher here in Mexico City, and a means of getting in touch.

My first attempt was a short visit to Sanborn's down the street, but I soon realized there was little chance Papi's work would be among the blockbusters the department store sold. If he was writing blockbusters, I'd have known it by now. I started to notice how many bookstores there were among all the shops jammed into the streets around our apartment. And then there were the flea markets. Aiyai! It was even more mind-boggling once I stepped into a micro-independent only to find shelves lining walls to the ceiling, aisles so narrow two people couldn't pass, and books piled in every available space. There were actually two whole walls of poetry. And this was just one store and one day.

I couldn't say I was being systematic about the search. But then, when had I ever bothered being systematic? I did look under Ruiz, then under Papi's mother's surname, Nebrija, assuming he'd have gone back to the double-barrelled form if he was in Mexico and was still writing. I found nothing. While I was standing in front of the *N*'s, I was struck by the title on the spine of another book. *Canto General* by Neruda. I pulled the book out. The Chilean poet had been one of Papi's favourite authors. This was the same edition as Papi's had been, I remembered the exact same cover hiding Papi's face as he read to us out loud. I flipped the book open. Mouthed the words as my eyes skimmed over them, memories of lying on my own or my sister's bed, the two of us rolled together in a quilt — two bugs in a rug our mother called us — listening as Papi read and the moon shone behind him. Only during Papi's storytime was Faith affectionate while still awake. She'd put her chubby arm under my head and let me snuggle close. From the security of her two extra years, she sistered me.

I looked back at the page the book had opened to. *Beautiful the hand or waist/that, enveloped by a fleeting moon, /saw the denizens of the deep tremble, /the wet elastic river of lives, /starry growth in fish scales, /seminal opal disseminated/in the ocean's dark sheet.* In my mind, not on the page, I saw a woman — dark, Mexican, reclining, asleep, eyes closed, breasts exposed, a loose tunic in rich colors flowing down her body, her legs, the moon cresting above her pillow, two moon shadows like reflections encircling her waist. I had never had a picture spring from words before. A gift from a poet to me? I flipped to another page. This time I clearly heard Papi's voice reciting Neruda in my head. *Because in my life, Mexico, you live like a little/lost eagle that circles in my veins.* The book was a gift. Or could be a gift. One I would give to Faith.

My gift-giving had always been directly proportional to my feelings for the gift in question. The giftee might decide they didn't like it, in which case they could always give it back to me. I'd even been known to read books before I gave them away as presents. Today I didn't have time though because Faith was home when I got back. A relatively healthy Faith, dressed to go out.

If Faith was surprised at the unexpected present, she covered up well. "I remember this," she said, turning the book over then back again. "One of our 'bedtime stories.' How about that." She laid one hand flat on the cover, then slid the book under the guidebook she'd slipped under her arm. There was an awkward minute's silence. "I was just on my way out. To do some exploring. Do you want to come along?"

"Well, I should really…," Faith didn't exactly look disappointed, but… Oh, I got it. An invitation in lieu of thanks. It was a good thing I'd inherited some of our mother's interpreting skills. Besides which, it was a relief to see Faith looking so healthy for once. Actually eager and able to take on some physical activity. "Sure."

As we walked, Faith pointed out the occasional sinking building. She gestured to our feet, where the lakes and canals used to be before the Spaniards built their empire on backfill. No wonder so many buildings collapsed during the big earthquake. Nothing and no one was on solid ground here. I remembered the leaning cathedral on the Zócalo and tasted again a spurt of coconut milk. I think I even blushed.

When we stopped to rest, eyes stinging from the afternoon smog, it was away from the noise of traffic, in Alameda Park. I closed my eyes and strained to hear the unfamiliar sound behind the occasional shout and laughter of children playing, adults calling out Aguas! – Watch out! – and chairs scraping on gravel – the sound of water running in a creek and the breeze through the tops of trees. Ash, poplar and

willow. Canadian trees. I contemplated nature with my eyes
firmly shut.

I didn't feel the slightest urge to pull out my sketchbook.
After a while, I sensed Faith get up and wander off. I stayed
motionless, moving inward through my mind's eye. I imagined that eye, wondered if it was the one — hidden in the
centre of my forehead — that just might allow me to see
properly one day.

"Hope. Hey, Hope." I told myself not to budge. Maybe
she'd go away. "Come on. There's something I want to show
you." I squeezed my eyes tight. "I've found this great
museum, right here in the park. With paintings by the same
artist as the one on Papi's book. Come and take a look." Faith
pulled on my arm.

I sighed — Faith said nothing — squinted, and looked
around. A toddler was chasing a flock of pigeons whose necks
bobbed furiously back and forth as they tried to outrun her.
The pigeons finally took wing just as they reached the fountain; the little girl pitched in headfirst. A nanny appeared, there
was scolding, crying, and the thrumming of pigeon wings.

I stretched out a hand to Faith to be pulled up, then
remembered her delicate state and pushed off the bench
myself. Faith led me to a building in a far corner of the park.
"Just look," she said. I did. At *A Sunday Afternoon Dream in the
Alameda Park* by Diego Rivera. The same left-of-centre artist
José had laughingly compared me to.

In Rivera's mural of the park, there was no burbling
stream or breeze, just scattered trees and scores of people filling up every available space. People alive and dead. I recognized a few figures from Mexico's past — Aztecs, workers, revolutionaries, musicians — all playing, fighting, strolling,
partying, arguing, sleeping. And just left of centre, a grinning
skeleton decked out in women's finery and an elaborate
headdress. Death itself, herself — Katrina — walking hand in
hand, arm in arm with a schoolboy Rivera.

Through colour, form, and shape he hinted at – no, blared out – the whole of Mexican history: comedy, tragedy, masks, and the naked truth.

I didn't believe in coincidence. This Alameda Park was so much more revealing than the one I had thought I'd seen or felt. I wanted Rivera's vision and the memories as mine, part of my cells, my unconscious, my heritage.

But I knew it wasn't just this one Mexican artist's vision I wanted to become mine. I craved a more personal vision, one Papi might have transmitted.

Sometimes I asked myself, what if Papi did return on his own, without being hunted down or dragged back? Could he ever make up for all those lost years?

The few times Papi punished us – for throwing snowballs wrapped around stones or setting fire to our makeshift sweat lodge – I ran crying to my room and plotted my future as a monster or a saint. Whichever would serve to hurt him the most. I wallowed in self-pity and anger until Papi came in to apologize, which he always did.

He never stopped at an apology though, he'd crack a joke, pull a face or twirl my hair into a topknot, anything to make me laugh. I was *mad* at him, dammit, but I'd laugh anyway. I hated myself for laughing, for letting him off.

Would it be the same thing now? If Papi came back, would he apologize? Without a smile, or a joke or a laugh this time? And would I forgive him on my own? Without having to be urged or coaxed? What words, no, what images would show him what he'd left behind?

José finally had my first 3D frame ready for me to work with in the studio. There was nothing stopping me now. But when I got to the studio that morning, it suddenly seemed impossible to work on a new painting without a fresh set of brushes. So I walked to the station, took the metro, and got off five stops later in front of the bargain art supplies store. Since I was out anyway, I went to the bank, the grocery store for snacks, the pharmacy, and the post office to buy stamps just in case. I came back to the studio and sat in front of my new canvas. Nothing. I decided it was music I needed to relax. But the snacks were where I'd left them by the boom box, and I realized I was hungry. So I sat out by the open door looking onto the alley, ate, watched the lizards climb the wall on the building across the way, and came back in to take a beer out of the cooler. That and the next one took another ten minutes.

Finally I sat down at the canvas, noticed a flea market shawl had fallen from its hanger, went and hung it up, and sat back down again. It was now 12:42 p.m., and I had done exactly diddlysquat.

I told myself this first attempt wouldn't be a keeper, quit feeling so anxious, you're free to do whatever the hell you want. Was that the problem after all, total freedom?

Just then, Anouk walked in and said hi.

As usual with me, my first impressions had been wrong. I remembered thinking Alan was the other artist from the studio I would relate to because of our New Worldness. Time had proved me wrong.

On her way back from the sink with two jars of water, Anouk stopped to have a look at my new canvas. "Interesting." She looked from the canvas to me. "We haven't seen a lot of you lately."

"Oh, I've been doing the tourist thing."

"But isn't your Dad Mexican?"

"Uh-huh."

"Do you live here with him?"

"No." Anouk kept waiting, expecting more. "He left us when I was fourteen."

"That's too bad." Anouk put a jar under her arm and rubbed the back of her neck with her freed hand. "Or I guess it depends. On what he was like. My dad's a real jerk. We'd have been better off without him."

It struck me then. Papi hadn't been a jerk. So it made no sense, believing he put his art before his family. Was the reason for his leaving to be found somewhere else? Before I could think it over some more or say anything in reply, Anouk said, "Could you give me some advice?"

She moved toward her easel and set down the jars. I followed. "I can try," I said.

Anouk was still into rocks, but now she'd added colour. "I was missing all the subtlety and play of light on surfaces." Anouk had spent time in a boarding school in England, which explained why her English was so good.

She pointed to her paper board. "See here. My background is overpowering the focus. I don't know how to get it right."

"Have you ever tried rubber cement?"

"Ages ago."

"I'll lend you some if you want."

It had been a long while since I worked with watercolours. It had been a long while since I'd been with someone I'd like to be able to call my friend.

Words came easily around Anouk. We had to wait for the cement outline to dry before she could paint the dark background. We talked while she tested for wetness, mixed colours for her palette and started to paint – talked about fathers, home, Mexico, and her kid. Finally she peeled away the dried cement to show a rock surrounded by a ring of muted red.

I went back to my easel and we worked in silence, side by side. I measured on my canvas the exact placement of the openings to be cut into it. Nine in all.

Faith swung by to pick me up since she was in Coyoacán anyway, having been on a sightseeing trip to Cortés's palace, and was taking me along on her next palace trip. I packed away my exacto knives; Anouk asked when I'd be in next. While we talked about days and times, Faith wandered through the studio, looking at each artist's wall.

The first thing Faith said when we stepped outside was, "I like her work best."

"Hmmm," I wasn't listening. I was thinking about fathers and jerks.

There was something I had to ask. I stopped in the middle of the sidewalk. Faith went on ahead a couple of steps before she realized I wasn't following her. She waited for me to catch up.

Fresh from being with Anouk, seeing how easily thoughts could be aired if given a chance, and how the word *father* didn't have to wear a warning DANGER AHEAD, I found the courage to blurt out the question first formed by my fourteen-year-old self, "Why did he go? Do you know?"

Faith looked taken aback, but she knew exactly what I was talking about. She glanced to either side, as if checking to see that no one was within earshot. Why such a taboo? Where did we get it from? "I... I just guessed he went crazy again."

"What do you mean, crazy?"

She looked at me as if I'd gone strange. "You don't remember?"

"Remember what?" I felt like yelling at her to hurry up and spit it out.

"That other time. Seven years before he left. I was nine. When he went all strange. Crazy. Sick in the head. I read that manic-depression can cycle in sevens. That was him. They took him away to the hospital. Mom always told us he was on a reading tour, a long reading tour, but I knew better. I heard them argue when he got back. He said he hated the hospital. He said he'd never go back. He said they'd stolen his self. Mom said he was forgetting something. She said his self was gone way before that. She said the hospital gave him his self back."

Me, seven, Papi, a frightening stranger. Papi asking me who I was. Papi yelling at the television. Papi opening the car door with the car still moving. Papi putting his fist through the front door. It was all there. It had all been there all along, just waiting to be called up. That first time and the last.

It was our first day back at school after Papi left. Faith and I taking off boots, tuque, and mitts in the main cloakroom, the two of us alone and early. A friend of mine walked in. I told her about the note, our father's leaving. Faith shot me a warning glance.

By lunchtime in the playground, I was friendless. The story had gotten around.

Faith and I walked home together that night. We trudged in silence through snowdrifts, took shortcuts so as not to be seen.

Silence then. Silence in between. Silence ever since. The cloak of protection when the world went amiss.

Anouk said her father was angry all the time. My father had been mad.

We went to the Palacio Nacional anyway. When silence was broken once, it must take an effort of will to break it again. We weren't practised enough. It was easier to admire Rivera's *Epic of the Mexican People in their Struggle for Freedom and Independence*. To think of only it for then.

Epic. I was dwarfed by the immensity of the painting. The mural started a foot above my head, then extended another twenty feet higher to just below the vaulted ceiling. My neck went into spasms from craning back so far. Or maybe it was the tremors Faith's words had set off in my brain.

She was staring unfazed. I elbowed her.

She shrugged me off, then turned to glare. "Tell me something. If you can't look at a work of art for more than a sum total of five minutes how do you ever expect to execute one? It's the same everywhere we go. Do you know how long this project took Rivera to complete? Do you? Sixteen years, that's how long. And *you* can't stand here for sixteen seconds. Give me a break."

Her tone brought me back to the present, freezing the tremors like liquid nitrogen. "What makes you so patient?"

Faith shot me a scornful look.

"No, really. I want to know. You're not an artist, so it's not the technique or the brush strokes or the colour combos. And I don't know how many words of Nahuatl you can get out of this. What is it?"

"If you really want to know, it's the music."

"Music?" I stopped and listened for a minute. Nothing. No piped-in sound. "What music?"

"In my head, you dolt. The score is laid out here, can't you see? Here," she pointed from the pre-Hispanic market, to the armoured Spaniards, the priests, the revolutionaries, fuming factories, the nuclear holocaust. "Look how it builds to a crescendo. The peaceful market, the invading armies, the uprising, the blood, the destruction. It's all there." She had my attention, but not my ear. Hers was not my sense, but her words projected me into the fresco anew, beyond the colours, the lines, and the shades. The artist had used his palate as he might have penned a song or written a poem. What a tragedy if his brush had been taken away before he was finished. For the space of a second, I heard both Papi's rhymes and my sister's tune.

"You know that Alameda mural? The one titled *A Sunday Afternoon Dream in Alameda Park*. Originally, Rivera wanted to call it *God Does Not Exist*." Faith said, her head thrown back.

Funny, for the first time in a long while I had a feeling He might.

Then again, I read once that music is the only thing that gives the mentally ill relief from hallucinations because it lets

the mind turn off and fills the vacuum with sound. I wondered whether Faith and I weren't both a little mad. It would
explain the music, wouldn't it?

My nightmare started innocently enough. I was racing a car
through traffic until I turned down a tree-lined avenue as
quiet as the other streets had been noisy. A banner was strung
between the line of trees in the centre of the avenue.
Madhouse Ahead, it said. In the distance I could see no
building, just a green fence with birds perched on top of each
pointed picket. As I slowed down, I realized the birds weren't
birds at all, but miniature faces leering and foaming at the
mouth. I stopped the car, stepped out, and immediately fell
back from the stench of vomit and curdled milk.

I scrambled back into the car, slammed the door behind
me and turned my back on the grimacing heads. When I
turned around again, I saw Papi.

My heart was pounding so hard as I jerked awake that I
was surprised José could sleep through it. But he snored softly,
one arm flung across his forehead. I had been sleeping at
José's more regularly lately, now that Faith seemed to be
recovering again. I took two big breaths and lay back down.

My mind wouldn't stop. Old stories came back to me:
How they'd both been in hospital when I was born. Mom to
deliver me and Papi… why? 0, 7, 14. A seven-year cycle,
Faith said. The losing of his self. Seven. Now I remembered.
The nightmares of long-limbed monsters that started a couple of months before my seventh birthday. Then I turned
seven. My mother pleading, "Pedro, what's going on?"
Soldiers marching across the TV screen, Papi yelling at us to
take cover. He couldn't distinguish between the screen and
real life. He was everywhere, on TV, in his body, and
nowhere, on the screen, in his mind. Mom driving him to his

appointment, dropping us off at school on the way, Papi in the passenger seat not knowing a car door was not an airplane flap. Open and shut. Open and shut. Papi so angry he put his fist through the front door. And then he was gone.

His return from that long, long "reading tour." The way the muscles around his mouth had forgotten how to turn up, only down. His smile when it reappeared was what ushered back my father. Seven years later, both he and his smile walked out of our lives.

The next morning, I asked José if he knew anything about mental institutions in Mexico. "Just that they're still in the Dark Ages. That's why the inmates are called melancólicos," was all he replied.

Mexican hospitals still believed in the effectiveness and safety of the old shock therapy: the controlled administration of electricity to the body to produce metabolic changes, smooth out the speeded-up highs and the despairing lows their patients go through. The old shock therapy, not the new and improved. That day I called every hospital in Mexico City asking for Pedro Ruiz, thankful every time I was told they had no patient by that name.

XII

Faith and I were in the Palacio de Bellas Artes, pretty well back where we'd started since the palace is across from Alameda Park. Only this time, Kiko was with us. The mysterious tutor. The man Faith saw every other day and whom I had never met. He didn't look at all the way I'd expected. He was quite tall and square-shouldered and nervous, constantly lifting his hands to hook his hair – long, black, and sleek – behind his ears. He had a crooked mouth that trembled slightly when he spoke.

Faith chose the Palacio for the works by Orozco and Siqueiros, but it turned out the stained glass windows interested her more. "Look at that."

Kiko answered, "Those are the volcanoes Ixtlacihuatl and Popocatepetl, the ones we can see from here on clear days." I hardly recognized the names spoken with a true Nahuatl accent. Kiko's Spanish, though, was unaccented; his voice in both Spanish and Nahuatl was soft and shook ever so slightly.

"A volcano." Faith said. "Maybe we'll get to see an eruption. Rivulets of liquid fire on the run."

Kiko smiled. "We could go visit them some day. Your chances aren't too good though. Ixtla is extinct and Popo is dormant. It hasn't erupted in seventy years."

"Too bad," Faith sighed. "It would still be worth a visit. That's where water comes from, you know, trapped in volcanic gases. The ash attracts and collects water droplets. Isn't that bizarre? I'd love to see a volcano up close."

I felt superior for half a minute. Faith *had* seen a volcano up close. She just didn't know it: Mont-Royal. Of course, the only reason I knew was because I once had a boyfriend who went to College Brebeuf and spent time in their research centre.

Personally, I couldn't see any reason to make a special trip to see a pile of dead rock, but I knew I'd have little say if Faith made up her mind. It was like she was driven these days to see and do everything she wouldn't be able to do once she was tied down with a baby. Or to squeeze everything in before – and if – her sick spells became more frequent.

Of course, I might think differently if I ever got to see an underwater volcano. The perfect breeding ground for coral reefs. Maybe that was what intrigued Faith, how something dead could come to life, rock transformed into lava, steam or ash or a breeding ground.

Kiko went on as though there'd been no interruption. "There are all kinds of legends about how the two volcanoes came to be. Some say they were an Aztec princess and her lover, a warrior who was sent by her father to bring back the head of an enemy to win her hand. While he was away, she died, thinking he'd been killed. When he came back from the war to find her dead, he laid her body out on a hill, lit an eternal torch, and knelt by her side. Both lovers turned to stone."

Faith was only half-listening because she had her nose in her guidebook. "It says that the village smack dab in the middle of the two volcanoes is Nepautta – Nepautta means 'in between' in Nahuatl – and was the birthplace of..."

"Oh, wow. Look at this." I'd spotted another Rivera. Faith turned to look, then returned to her book. "That painting was originally commissioned for the Rockefeller Center in New York, but walled over because of this." She pointed to Lenin's face looming in the centre above the giant telescope and microscope, workers demonstrating on either side. "Rivera redid this version afterwards from scratch. I wonder if people in New York realize it when they walk past that blank surface now. If only walls could speak."

"It's a good thing for us they don't," I said. "There'd be no way to keep a secret otherwise."

It was a joke. I didn't understand why Faith blanched and took a step backward to steady herself.

"What's wrong?" I put both hands on her shoulders and felt her lean into me. I almost stumbled. Kiko took a step forward.

"I... I don't know. I feel... dizzy."

I slid an arm around her back and craned my neck looking for a chair. All I could see was the flight of marble stairs. I helped Faith ease down onto the second step then sat next to her. Light was streaming in through the Tiffany stained glass window, bisecting the two volcanoes, hitting the spot where we'd been standing. For a second, I watched the play of light and colour as from a great distance then shook myself.

"Maybe you're suffering from heatstroke," I groped for a logical explanation. "Or the baby's done a somersault."

Faith didn't bother responding, just kept taking big gulps of air, and looking ghostlike. People didn't even glance at us as they slipped by. I looked up at Kiko. "I... I think I'd better go find a wet paper towel."

"Of course, I'll sit with her." His long legs folded down into a crouch. He leaned his head into Faith's, one hand at the nape of her neck, the other one resting in her lap. It was a practised touch. I realized I knew nothing about the time they spent together, nothing about what they had.

I hated to leave her. A sense of foreboding had invaded every pore, every sense, every thought I had. Invisible but there in the grumblings in my chest, in the dull pain at the

small of my back, in the hairs along my arms that refused to
lie flat.

*Dreamt my womb was a Hope painting. Oil on canvas with a little
door to the inside. I turned the knob my bellybutton forms. Reached in.*

*Inside no placenta, no blood, no organs. No crystal balls or brass keys
either. Just a tiny hand. Clutching my baby finger. Tapping Morse code
on my palm. I read the code. I read her words. "Don't go."*

Faith had been bedridden for a week. Coincidentally, for that
same week we'd been awakened not by the dogs' barking, but
by the mourning of doves.

I didn't believe in coincidence. I was no longer worried,
I was scared.

The call of the mourning dove had an insistent eeriness
to it that echoed not in my head but in my chest. An under-
ground rumbling that never ever stopped. My days were reg-
ulated by the persistent pulsing of the pigeon's call. Here
people say it's not the pigeons at all, but La Dolorosa crying
through the streets. Some say she's La Malinche come back
to haunt the Spaniards, or the ghost of a poor woman from
pre-Columbian times.

Whatever the source, it was to the beat of that same soft
throbbing that I dialled my mother's number, waiting after
each rotation for the dial to make its slow way back. I felt like
using the magic formula from my childhood, reserved for
those times when Faith and I desperately wanted Mom's permission or help, "Maman chérie adorée." Mother, light of my
life, love of my heart, grant me one wish, and there'll be no
more. Children are much better at psychology than adults. I
didn't use psychology on her this time, reverse or otherwise,
I just sent out a plea.

When do mothers lose the ability to set everything right? Never, according to José. Witness, he said, the Virgin Mother. José could say things like that without looking the least bit uncomfortable.

That's what I loved about him. That and the fact he was colour-blind. I got to translate the colours of the world to him. He translated the invisible to me.

Back home in Quebec, I didn't know anyone who would own up to believing in the Virgin Mary – chalice and tabernacle are swear words for Christ's sake – let alone count on the Holy Mother to set things right. I couldn't imagine a woman who would own up to having slept with only one man in her life, her husband, let alone owning up to not having slept with any man whatsoever to be with child. But José was not from Quebec.

I didn't tell him what my nickname used to be. I was like Mom in that, after Papi left – one day he was there, the next he was gone, what was stopping the same thing from happening again? – my worrying reached new heights.

I worried about everything. I couldn't trust the world to do anything right. When all my friends but me had started their periods, I was convinced I was pregnant. Not having even kissed a boy at that point, the odds were pretty slim, but that didn't faze me, "There's been one virgin birth, why not two?" On one especially angst-ridden night, I confessed my fears to Faith and from then on, she insisted on calling me Mother Mary. Mom never knew why.

Anyway, not having José's familiarity with the real Virgin Mother, I called on my own mother instead.

She arrived that same day. By bus. Her trip was without incident, unlike our trip with the ridiculous menacing man and the fear he inspired.

But that fear had been nothing like this. The fear this time was more invasive. There was no culprit to point to, only this nameless, painless poisoning.

What I needed was some kind of cleansing ritual to flush the poison out.

José came up with the rite I needed. The two of us were standing at the foot of Faith's sickbed. Mom was bustling and clucking and doing a good job of being annoying enough to make me forget Faith's illness. Reality has a way of undercutting one's illusions. For me, reality set in the minute my mother arrived as she whipped off the heating pad – our version of chicken soup – perched on the mound of Faith's belly. Faith was lying more or less in the same position, boca arriba, the sheets bunched up at the foot of the mattress, sweat rolling down her cheeks.

"Good heavens, Hope," Mom cried, "A heating pad! In this weather! What about my poor little granddaughter! She's going to think she's in incubator hell!" As good an introduction to the world as any if you asked me.

José's arrival was a welcome distraction. When he stepped into the room, I ran a finger down his arm in greeting. Kiko must have let him in. Kiko had taken to dropping over at odd hours to sit by Faith's side and hold her hand while our mother eddied round them.

Mom looked up, "José, how nice. Can I offer you anything? Lemonade…"

José nodded at Faith. At Faith, whose illness he had once written off as hypochondria. Luckily, Faith never knew both José and I had doubted her. She didn't know the two of us owed her an apology.

José turned his smile on Mom. "No, that's fine Señora Alder. I just dropped by on my way to the basilica to light a candle for Faith and the baby."

"Now, isn't that nice, José," she said. "I don't set much store in all that myself, but what do I know?"

Kiko walked in carrying a bowl of fresh fruit, the only food Faith seemed able to eat. "What's up?" he asked.

"José's off to light a candle for Faith and the baby."

Kiko stopped in his tracks, almost letting the bowl drop. "Something wrong?" our mother asked.

"Gotten religion all of a sudden, have you?" Kiko said. "We'll see how much help you get."

We all stared. Kiko placed the bowl on the bedside table, paused, then straightened up, "Sorry. Guess I've just seen too many effects of religious overkill."

There was an awkward silence.

Faith rarely talked about Kiko. But I remembered one day listening to the news of uprisings in Chiapas and her repeating something Kiko had said. How when violence has been done to you, violence grows in your heart.

Our mother gave Kiko a long appraising look. Then she bent down to pick up the washcloth that had fallen to the floor, turned the washcloth over to the still-clean side, and put it back on Faith's forehead. "My experience has mostly been that prayers go unanswered too, Kiko. But then I've never been to light a candle to the Virgin of Guadelupe." She smiled, first at Kiko then at José.

José looked surprised. My mother continued smoothly, "How could I live in Mexico for so many years and not know the story?"

Listening to our mother, who of course didn't need any encouragement to launch into the story for Faith and me – just as well since it broke the tension in the air – I had a clear image of Juan Diego, the peasant to whom the Virgin appeared a few centuries ago. Weathered hat in hand, peasant cloak draped over his shoulders, the same cloak on which the Virgin left her rose-petal-stamped likeness as proof of her coming. Or rather I had a clear image of Juan Diego as modelled by José, whose conviction right now was big enough to convince me if not the multitudes.

Kiko had pulled up a chair at the head of Faith's bed. He interrupted our mother, something rare for him. In fact, it might even have been a first. "You know, in the people's eyes, the miracle wasn't the apparition of the Virgin Mary, as interpreted by Juan or the priests. Once the story was told and retold, the true significance of the likeness on the cloak was seen and its message of hope received by the whole nation, especially at that time when an Aztec revolution was brewing. The woman who came to him had coppery skin and dark eyes. The woman pictured was greater than the moon she stood on and wore the cloak of an ambassador bearing messages from the Aztec god of the Sun. She was the Aztec Mother Goddess, the Dark Virgin. The stars on the cloak reproduced the exact formation of the constellations in the sky on the night of the day she came to Juan. The black sash was the same as the one worn by all pregnant women of that time. All were reminders of the virgin birth of the Sun god whose messenger she was. It was that woman and her promise of protection for the Aztec people that convinced them to adopt her as their patron saint."

"Really? I didn't know that."

I let Kiko and our mother debate the finer points of interpreting a miracle as I began to work out how I would paint José. I'd need a sheet dipped in plaster draped around his shoulders, or should the draping stand alone? No, better to drape it around José, stamped with the image left by the Virgin, dark or white, whichever she was, for Juan to offer as proof to the priests. I'd put candles on the floor at José's feet – candles we'd made with the market kids – on stools, on my bench, on wall-mounted shelves to add light, shadow, depth. Then I'd paint Mexico's past and maybe, just maybe, I'd paint my own miracle.

I broke in on Mom and, looking at José, responded to his earlier announcement, "I'll go with you." Mom looked nonplussed. I usually let her ramble, without interruption. I usually liked it when she rambled, it meant I could lose myself in my own thoughts and not have to give any direction to the flow of words. But not right now. She was taken aback at first, but within moments was saying, "Of course, why not? Go, go."

So we did.

The drive took forever. Theoretically, the basilicas were part of Mexico, but they were on its very northernmost fringe. Between rush hour, which turned the main axes into one big parking lot, and the needle on the dash flickering to either side of empty, I thought we'd never get there. We had to line up in the street at the gas station, cars behind honking for us to get a move on, cars ahead waiting like us to fill up on Magna Sin. Magna Sin. Ironic, given our destination, but I wasn't sure José would appreciate the irony so I kept quiet.

José and I didn't speak on the drive there. The sense of foreboding was still with me. If I'd known how to pray, I would have, to anyone or anything. I was glad he couldn't read my thoughts. There was something sacrilegious about suggesting praying to just anything. Which was probably why I painted instead of prayed.

I realized within seconds of walking into the New Basilica that there would be no miraculous conversion for me there. José pointed us toward the ugly new blockhouse building instead of the old church at its side, explaining that because of the crowds who come to view the cloak, the government decided to build the new facility — with a capacity of ten thousand — and transfer the garment there.

"You'd have to come back next week for the full impact. December 12th is the anniversary of the day the Virgin appeared to Diego. Thousands and thousands of people make a pilgrimage here, some on their knees."

I told him I'd pass, thank you very much. This set-up was quite tacky enough.

Inside the cavernous hall, José wove through the crowd
as he led me over to the nearest wall and its hundreds of
flickering candles. On closer inspection, I realized the flickering didn't come from actual flames. The candles were fake,
with little electric tubes inside. Drop a coin in the slot in
front of the candle and its bulb lit up. I tried three different
candles, and not a single one worked. I looked halfheartedly
for a coin return.

José – maybe fearing that the implications of a candle
refusing to light might sink in – took my elbow and sta-
tioned us in the slowly shuffling line of people, then pro-
pelled me forward onto the next modern miracle. A moving
sidewalk. In a church! I avoided looking at José.

Holding onto the guiderail I watched incredulously as
we were transported down the length of the basilica and
around its centrepiece, the miracle cloak, enshrined in its
own altar, glowing as we passed underneath.

"You've got to be kidding," I finally turned toward José.
He didn't look put out, just amused.

"We need all the divine intervention we can get," he
said. "'So far from God, so close to the United States' as they
say." He lifted his toes up as the magic carpet ran out and
came to a full stop while I skipped onto the floor and kept
walking. He hurried to catch up. "But this is just the side-
show. Now for the real reason we're here. Come on over to
the old basilica."

It was true I had newfound appreciation for the reverence
an old, ornate church could inspire. The vaulted ceiling, the
stained glass windows, the carvings for the Stations of the
Cross, the altar. Reverence but not belief. I felt no miracle
whispers as José knelt at my side in the middle pew, bowed
his head, made the sign of the cross, and began to pray. I
closed my eyes. Nothing. I looked up again, at the multi-
coloured patterns the fading light threw onto the walls. Made
a mental note to return some day to inspect the works of art.

Once we were back outside in the rapidly fading light of day, José pulled me close, "We could take Faith to a curandera too, you know. The old Otomí faith healer my family used to go to lives here with her daughter now. I'm sure I could track her down. You'll see, we'll take care of Faith. She'll be better prontito, you'll see."

Pronto. Soon. Or reasonably soon. Prontito, very soon. Or a little bit longer. Prontitito, improbably soon. And prontititito impossibly soon. I tried to pretend that my pores could still breathe.

XIII

They quote the Buddha to me. Life is suffering, they say, don't go thinking you have any power to stop the suffering. All you can stop is your wild mind.

My wild mind. I come from a family of crazy people. It's in our blood, in our genes. I have resisted for years; that should be worth something in the grand scheme of things. And am resisting still, though some days are tougher than the rest.

A sleeping pill, an anti-depressant, an upper, a downer, none of these will cross my lips. I will keen, I will rail, I will whimper instead. In weakness lies my strength.

This entry wasn't in Faith's handwriting. It wasn't even an entry. It was a handwritten scrap of paper taped onto a page that was blank except for today's date written in Faith's hand in the top right corner.

I eased out of a crouch, the sheaf of paper still in my hand. Soon Faith would have to find another hiding place; the number of pages in her journal would be too thick to fit behind the pipes. Plus it was getting harder and harder for her to get out of bed. I leaned back against the tub for a closer look.

The script was nearly illegible. None of the letters were fully formed, they spilled into each other, becoming a jagged blur. Where had I seen that handwriting before?

I lifted up the corner of the page and saw the tiny roll of scotch tape holding it in place. I lifted a bit further, with one finger just under the tape so it wouldn't rip. The tape came off easily.

By careful insistence, I freed all four corners and could flip the page over. Faith had written on the back, "Papi, 1983."

Slowly I turned the page around and ran my finger across the lines. Now I recognized Papi's handwriting, more frantic than that on the few scraps I had found in the days after Papi left, scraps I kept. Mine were his shopping lists, instructions, hellos and good-byes. But this. 1983. How many months or days or hours was this written before he disappeared? So much more telling than his official note, the one Mom kept – *Tengo que irme. Les amo. Discúlpenme.* I have to go. I love you. Forgive me.

This almost sounded like a poem he'd write, but he never wrote poetry longhand. He always said he wrote poetry like a musician, playing on his Selectric – his grand piano – the score to accompany the lyrics of his poems. He left his Selectric at home. As well as the uppers, the downers, the Lithiums, the Valiums. He'd gone off like Buddha stripped of his possessions, his life's work, his family, his friends.

In weakness lay his strength.

In Faith's weakness I saw no strength. She found none with us either. Her condition got so bad she finally let us take her back to the American hospital. The doctors there knew her already, they confirmed for us what she had known all along. This wasn't morning sickness or hypochondria or an over-active mind. This was cancer. My zodiac sign. Now we were the ones they were interested in. They took our blood, tapped our spines, and started proceedings to track down Papi, who would, if found still alive, be tapped and poked and perhaps pronounced useless just like us.

The next decision was to visit the curandera, a decision that didn't come easily. Faith was afraid of another violation, another striptease in front of strangers. But Kiko had experience with curanderas, and his confidence decided her. My mother was afraid of the curandera's power, but she would do whatever Faith wanted. I must just have been afraid. But somehow reading Papi's words spurred me out of fear and into action. A good thing come from bad.

The curandera spoke Nahuatl. I was no help, nor was Mom, the professional interpreter. She spoke only Spanish, English, and French. So the healer's patient, Faith, had to help us decipher the old woman's instructions.

Faith lay naked on a cot, watching as the curandera prepared her dye. The old woman hammered with a stone pestle at the mixture inside first one, then another crude ceramic bowl. Without planning to, I had made a mental note of the quantity of shredded jagua fruit she used to make juice and the amount of ashes she stirred in for each of the two colours, ochre and russet. A professional tick. I was always looking for additions to my palette.

But then I forgot about colour combinations, mixing techniques, and the reason we were there. I was struck for the first time by Faith's lack of self-consciousness. Not because there was a stranger present, the withered woman whose broad smile didn't seem to promise too much healing magic that I could see – couldn't she have saved her own teeth? But because of anyone's presence, mine and our mother's not least of all. Growing up, Faith never let anyone see her naked: Mom, Papi, or me. She was always clutching a towel, a housecoat, or a shower curtain to her body.

Yet since Faith had joined me in Mexico, she hadn't thought twice about throwing off the old T-shirt to sleep naked, modelling nude for me, or seeing my paintings of her under public gaze. How could I have forgotten the way she used to be ashamed of the folds and the curves?

Somehow I didn't think Mexico's heat accounted for the change. Maybe it was because she was two now instead of one.

Faith scrunched up her nose in an effort to make sense of the woman's staccato Nahuatl words. I hadn't seen her do that in a long time. Teachers used to love it. In Secondary II math, the teacher said, "Oh, you're Faith's younger sister. A bright girl that one. She was my litmus test in class. Whenever her face puckered up, I could be sure at least 95 percent of the class didn't know what I was getting at, and it was time to start all over again." After Papi left, though, she learned not to give herself away. Until now.

Faith was not a natural interpreter, not like Mom. The fact that Mom seemed to have no words today was shocking in itself, enough to make me wonder if she wasn't the invalid. Faith caught one out of every five or ten words the curandera pronounced, so our comprehension – Mom's and mine – was sketchy at best. Luckily, the curandera matched actions to her words as Faith translated.

"The paint… the dye… catches in the… the thingies…" (the thingies!) "carved on the tube," the curandera brandished a stone roller with what looked like paper dolls cut out on it, this must have been the tube, "and is… transmogred to the skin." Was there such a word as *transmogred*?

I didn't listen to Faith's halting translation for a minute, just watched the lines in her face smooth out then bunch up again in sync with her efforts at concentration.

"The images protect evil" (Pardon me?) "no… heal." Faith's translation reminded me of a story our mother told, how an early Protestant translation of the Bible read "Thou shalt commit adultery" instead of "shalt not" and how another incompetent biblical translator had translated "let the children come unto me" by "But Jesus said unto her, let the children first be killed." That bungled version came to be known as the Murderer's Bible.

The curandera stepped back and inspected the track of stylized ochre figures she'd laid across Faith's belly, bisecting her protruding navel. She laid two other tracks on either side of the first, then made a motion as though handing the roller over to me.

I thought this was her job. Just like it had been the doctors' job up until now. The curandera insisted.

My hands guided the roller across Faith's flesh. The dolls, hands joined, marched across her sternum. In the background, the curandera murmured incantantions, spells, recipes, mathematical formulae, who knew? Faith quit interpreting, looked down, then up at me through twin eyes, and smiled.

I had never before had a canvas smile at me. Had a canvas warm to the touch, gentle with down, pliable under pressure. Had never before practised art with a mission. At the curandera's bidding, my mother cradled the first shallow clay bowl full of dye by my side.

This was what we could do, my mother and I. Useless according to the doctors, but not in the curandera's eyes.

The ritual became part of our daily routine: stencilling onto Faith's body and that of her baby hidden under the swollen mother mound a chain of linked figures dancing with every move Faith made, with every kick the baby gave. As the tracking down of Papi became part of the doctors' routine. But I no longer wasted my hopes on him. I took action.

The night after the curandera's ritual I had another nightmare of a visit from the mad. I woke from it swaying. The hammock I'd strung up by Faith's bed was alive. I must have struggled in my sleep, unused to my new perch. I looked over for Faith, who was too ill for me to sleep by her side. She lay lifeless and white.

I jumped out of the hammock, grabbed Faith's shoulders and snatched my hands away, horrified at the feel of deadened flesh. I shook her first once, then twice, "Faith, wake up!"

She woke up immediately, confused and angry, and I felt like a fool. Only then did I remember the game we used to play as kids: left palms touching then running the fingers of our right along the backs of the two joined hands to get an eerie dead feeling. Our exploring fingers expected to feel sensation on both sides when it was possible only on one. That was the mistake I'd made, thinking I could feel my flesh in hers.

"What is it? What's wrong?" Her voice croaked.

"I… I'm sorry. I didn't mean to. It was a dream."

She fell back onto the pillow, closed her eyes. "Oh. A dream." Pause. "What about?"

"Nothing. Go back to sleep."

I lay down and looked up at the ceiling. Sticker stars and planets glittered neon green. Mom bought them so Faith would have something to look at when she got sick of lying in bed. She got the idea from our old dentist, but Mom's decorations were much more educational than his. She had me position the planets in order from the sun outwards then the successive phases of the moon. She even tried to have me line the stars up by constellation. But my arms were too tired by that time. How did Michelangelo ever do the Sistine Chapel?

I wasn't sure Faith fully appreciated the night display yet. Her only comment when Mom left the room was, "There goes our damage deposit."

XIV

A night of broken sleep didn't seem to have worsened Faith's condition. She was feeling stronger, in fact, strong enough to leave her bed and her pseudoconstellation-watching. She even felt strong enough to stand in front of the sink while Mom washed her hair. Mom was determined there were to be no lice incidents while she was there.

"I used to hate this so much." Faith's voice came out all choppy as Mom's fingers vibrated through her scalp.

"Did you?" she said. "You never said a thing." She grabbed the pitcher full of lukewarm water on the counter and poured from nape to forehead. Water cascaded down.

Water is the most difficult element to draw. It has no beginning or end. Each drop both individual and indivisible. Faith tried to explain to me once the similarities between water and the quantum theory. Something about how all matter had two defining but opposite traits: it could be both particles and waves at one and the same time. She tried to describe an experiment: two electrons being sent off in totally different directions, in time and in space, and yet forever remaining linked as part of one invisible wave. She gave up.

Mom said, "Maybe it's just as well you couldn't go snorkelling at Xihuatanejo. If you don't like water on your face."

Faith had to pause for the waterfall to stop before she could continue. "No, that's not it. I don't have anything against getting wet. It's having to do it in a sink. Having to take my bath in Hope's dirty bath water was bad enough but penny-pinching to the point where only my hair got washed in the kitchen sink was too much. The whole time I'd feel like retching just imagining all the peelings, leftovers, sour milk, and rotting lettuce that had been dumped down that drain. Oh, I've got to stop talking about it or I'll make myself gag all over again." A moment's pause. "What makes you think of Xihuatanejo?"

Mom squirted some conditioner into her hand. "Just an idea I had. That maybe, when you've had the baby and are feeling stronger, maybe all four of us could go back again." As though by giving birth, Faith would magically get better. At least she would finally let the doctors give her her treatment then.

Faith too pretended that all we were waiting for was the delivery. "Maybe there are volcano reefs there. If I can't see a volcano on land, at least I could see one in the sea. Ouch! Watch my eyes." Faith rubbed her eyes with both hands, then let Mom push her head back below the tap. "Hope says snorkelling is a blast."

Mom turned to me, "So you did like it, Hope? I'm never sure with you." She paused. I was glad to turn my mind to something else. Especially snorkelling.

"It was... incredible. Another world, all those living ribbons of colour in perpetual motion. Schools of fish travelling as one, hovering, swimming, doing an about-face. The surgeonfish, the parrotfish, the damselfish taking on all comers."

Mom broke in, "No schools for them." Faith had wrapped a towel around her head, turban style, and was pulling a chair out at the table as I washed out the sink. "They're real loners, it's true. Funny thing though. Even though they fight off anyone or anything that tries to invade

their territory, no matter how big, they do make a conces-
sion for neighbouring damsels who patrol a common border
with them. They help each other out sometimes to make an
invader beat a retreat. Because of that, I've heard them called
extended families, families of 'dear enemies.'"

I hadn't finished yet. "As I was saying," I interrupted,
clearing my throat while I turned off the tap, "Snorkelling
was incredible. We even saw a squid gliding along the ocean
floor. And floating... It felt like I was being held up not just
by water but by all the plankton, the plants, the fish. It's
like... like being in a cradle. Instead of a lullaby, just one
sound, the rasp of one breath going in, the next one out. And
nothing, nothing else."

Faith leaned back and said softly, "Maybe that's what it's
like for her inside." She looked down, touched her stomach.
"A watery cradle." She gave a small laugh. "Minus the plankton and the squid."

She looked determined all of a sudden, "We have to go
back there."

I suddenly remembered one of her journal entries about
her endless baths. *In the water, I, like Sonnie, am suspended, as
near weightless as can be. I crave more moments of otherworldliness.*
Sonnie. What a name for a girl.

I was sure Faith didn't even realize what she was doing
when she chose the name. All my life, she'd complained
about the handles Mom had saddled us with, and yet she'd
gone and done the same thing with her daughter-to-be. The
way I saw it, Faith – knowing she'd have to be both mother
and father to her child – had decided, subconsciously, that
her child too would learn to take on both properties of the
daughter and the "son." A male "sun" to the female moon.

Then again, maybe she just thought it had a kind of
happy sound.

Mom's voice broke in on my thoughts. "Of course, we
will. The baby, too, as I said. I've heard newborns are natural

swimmers. Until they're three months old. We'll take her swimming in the sea. Just the three of us." Woman–womb–water. Together. "We'll be damselfish." I didn't have the heart to tell her the bad news that the damselfish were male. What did it really matter anyway? Maybe they had been female at another point in their lives.

Since I'd been in Mexico, water was an element that kept wanting to imprint itself on my art. In Montreal, the element was every bit as present, but somehow I only explored it in the form of snow or ice. Working in studios back home, I didn't remember noticing the way sweat formed then trickled down between a model's breasts in the hot summer months. When I thought of skin, goosebumps were what came to mind. Big Canada geese. The makeshift studios – garages, tool sheds, abandoned sugar shacks – which were the only kind I could afford to go in on, always had to be outfitted with a view to the long winter months: primitive heating systems installed, wide aluminum pipes from Canadian Tire lined up end to end, hung from the ceiling, two holes cut out above the place where the model sat. The model was more often windswept than perspiring from the blasts of heat. We artists had to wear anoraks and fingerless gloves at our stations outside the radius of warmth.

Mom half-laughed as she unwrapped the cord from around the hairdryer and plugged it in. "Faith and the kitchen sink." I'd forgotten. That was how all this got started. "You always were the princess, we supplied the pea. The meagre royalties of a poet weren't enough to keep you in style, even less the starvation wage of an interpreter for refugees…"

I'd seen Mom at work with her clients back home. People thought community interpreters were only there to translate, but when a woman had been tortured in her own country, a visit to the doctor's could be a horrendous ordeal, stirring up memories of torturers and executioners. The same with a day in court. When the country a man harked from dragged him through kangaroo court and sentenced him to death for a crime he didn't commit, a refugee hearing in Canada was not likely to inspire confidence. To help her clients confide in a doctor or speak the truth to a refugee panel, it took hours and hours of background work. Unpaid a lot of the time. Which showed where society's priorities lay. The highest-paid professionals in the medical field were dermatologists. Now there was a life-enhancing skill.

Faith's hair billowed out under the blowdryer's force, making her look like Medusa. I banished the urge to make a sketch of her with snakes in the place of hair; she was still mad at me over the python in the marketplace. She ran up one side of me and down the other when she spied my finished painting, going on about my responsibility to consider the symbolism attached to the images I used. "Your painting gives me the creeps." I tried to tell her we were in Mexico now, where snakes were a force for good, a symbol of the Great Mother, a source of strength, and a symbol of life mastery. But then I remembered the meaning of a snake that isn't mastered: death and chaos.

Mom didn't need to read people's private diaries or correspondence to learn their inner secrets. Her technique consisted in talking their ear off for hours at a time, then suddenly falling silent. The response was always the same. Her listener was so stunned by the silence, the lull in the torrent of words, and so relieved to actually hear the sound of his or her own voice when they dared test it out that words came tumbling unbidden.

Yet at the same time, a woman who talked so much had silenced the words that really counted. Out of the false belief she was protecting us? To spare us the hurt of the truth? Mom gave chase to any verb or any noun that might penetrate the curtain of silence she'd erected around Papi's leaving. Like a damselfish, pursuing any intruder that approached its small grazing field, its refuge, its dormitory, and its nest.

Now Faith's hair was sleek and dry. Mom twirled it between her fingers, creating three separate strands that she started working into a braid with the skill of a weaver at her loom.

I'd almost forgotten what we were talking about a second time when Faith spoke up, "What royalties? It's not like Papi ever contributed that much."

"Damn." One of the strands dropped; Mom had to let all three strands go. "Now I have to start all over again."

Faith raised her eyebrows at me. I waited.

"You're wrong," her fingers started up again but her eyes were focused elsewhere. "But maybe you got that idea from me." She picked up the elastic from the table. "I liked knowing that if anything happened, I could cope. Mom didn't have that. Her generation was so dependent on their men. When I was little, I used to be afraid something would happen to your grandpa. It seemed to me we'd be lost without him. I didn't want that to happen to us. Maybe I went to the other extreme. I made sure I met your every need. You girls always ran to me to show off your latest accomplishment or your latest bo-bo – remember that's what you called them. I was always there with praise and Band-Aids. Or to talk about the latest betrayal or crush or teacher. I never suggested you let your father kiss it better. I was too intoxicated with my own strength to realize strength is something to be shared."

Mom stopped, fumbled for an elastic, wrapped it three times around Faith's braid. Her voice dropped lower, "Maybe that's why he left. Because he thought we had no need for a husband or a father."

If we didn't need him then why, ever since, had our family felt like a wounded animal limping on three legs, its centre of balance forever lost? Papi used to joke and call us an entity unto ourselves. Or his inspiration: Faith, Hope, and Charity. Or sometimes his tres Gracias. Mom would always say "the three Graces were sisters" just to hear him state she looked young enough to *be* our sister. She always said that was why she married a Mexican: she never tired of the flattery. The only Canadian she'd ever heard refer to the three Graces called them Grace, Disgrace, and Candle Grease.

But who was Papi? Why did memories of him not include the man "come from a family of crazy people?" What had I blocked out? In the same way Mom chased the words that might bring our family tumbling down, had I gone one step further and chased away even the thoughts? I only remembered the commonplace, the stuff of every day, not a man who jumped into TV screens or flew a plane while still on the ground. I remembered the Papi who didn't hand out Band-Aids and was more likely to say "Buck up" than "poor dear." But who held my head, washed my hair when I was sick.

When Mom was away and Papi was the cook, he, Faith, and I dined on prairie oysters, a recipe he'd learned from one of his prairie-born artist friends. His prairie oysters not bull testicles but Premium crackers with a wall of butter around the four perimeters and a blob of ketchup or, for himself, hot sauce on the inside. A good thing Mom was never away for long stretches of time, although I guess the presence of starch (cracker), dairy (butter), and vegetable (tomato ketchup or red pepper hot sauce) – or was a tomato a fruit? – could qualify our diet as healthy to a certain degree.

Even on "ladies' nights," those cold winter nights when the three of us, Faith, Mom, and I, headed for our parents' bed, each with a book, an agreed-upon easy-listening tape (easier than what Faith would have chosen on her own, anyway) inserted in the alarm clock on the bedside table – warm bodies, legs intertwined, pages turning, flannel sheets, me sandwiched between the two of them – Papi was the one to bring us hot chocolate with miniature marshmallows floating on top. From the place assigned to me because my body generated the least heat and so, the others claimed, was better able to withstand their twinned warmth, I sweated freely, warm flesh beside me, hot liquid coursing down my throat. After Papi left, our ladies' nights came to an end.

Faith and I used to be close. We had to be; we could never sort out whose childhood was whose, which life story was which. Mom's memories of us as girls overshot the borders of our individual lives. In her view, we were most often just "the girls." Interchangeable. Faith's first words or first steps could just as easily have been mine. Papi remembered us separately if in rhyme. But that memory now was gone.

Our chores didn't change once Papi disappeared: Mom still washed the laundry, I sorted, Faith folded. Faith had the gift of creating orderly piles out of rumpled towels, shirts, and sheets. I didn't. Mom cooked, Faith washed, I dried unless Faith had a papercut or a hangnail. Such a wimp. She always made me clean the sink out first – the whole gagging routine again – even when she washed. She could never stand the touch of soggy meat, wilted lettuce, ground eggshells. I was much more tactile than she.

Papi shovelled the stairs and the front walk. In Montreal's winters, that was a full-time job. Snow piled so high we couldn't see over the top. Papi had to lift his arms higher and higher to deposit his shovelfuls. He learned the skill well for a man who'd grown up never seeing, tasting, or touching snow. You'd have sworn it was his birthright. When we were little, he'd bundle Faith and me up in our snowsuits – an exercise requiring a ten-minute struggle at least – hoods raised, scarves bound tightly around forehead and mouth, hands clumsy in awkward mitts, and we'd crazy carpet down the mini-hills he created for us. He built us little thrones in the snowbank when we were tired. There we sat and watched him work.

In the spring, he planted flowers, in the summer, he mowed our tiny front lawn, in the fall he raked leaves. He was a man of the outdoors. Not the great outdoors, not a hunter, a fisherman, a backpacker but a sun-worshipper, a wind expert, an explorer of urban parks, with us to guide. A reef dweller, not one for the open seas.

The silence stretched forever until Faith said, "Or maybe I was the trigger."

God, I couldn't believe it. We all blamed ourselves. Even worse, had we all blamed each other? I suddenly saw the importance of the "give" in "forgive" and how the gift of forgiveness was one we needed: Faith, me, Mom, Papi.

"Don't you remember Luc and Rémi?"

It came back then. Two of Faith's friends who'd gotten into the habit of sneaking over to the house whenever Mom and Papi were out. At sixteen Faith was still too young in Papi's books to date. No boys, no phone calls, no nothing. One night, Papi must have felt something was up. He and Mom left for the movies in the car, but he circled around the block in time to catch the boys just starting up the stairs to the front door. The moment he saw them he gunned the engine, raced down the street, and ran right up over our patch of lawn to the foot of the steps, the boys slipping and sliding to get away, Papi's car door half-open, his leg half-out, his voice – not in halves – bellowing out for all to hear at the trespassers on his territory, Mom frozen solid in the passenger seat, Faith and I staring wide-eyed from the balcony, waiting for a fist through the door.

"I hated him then," Faith whispered. "I really did."

She went on, "But I don't really think that's what it was. I think he was afraid of losing himself again." She looked at Mom, knowing she was acknowledging something that had never been spoken. Papi's illness. "And becoming that stranger we would learn to hate."

I remembered the morning after he left, Mom still holding the note, Faith's voice trailing off as she tried to get Mom to talk. I headed to the front hall closet, threw on my parka and moon boots, jerked the door open, grabbed the shovel, half-slid down the stairs, and set to work. Sweat trickled between my half-formed breasts, a muscle cramped in my left shoulder, my gloveless hands turned red then white. Soon I couldn't see past the walls of snow. Atonement.

My turn. "What does it matter why he left? What I want to know is where is he now?"

Mom said as though it were fact, "He came home. To Mexico."

"Or maybe he got sick." Faith spoke. There was silence. Mom stiffened then dropped her hands to Faith's shoulders.

"Let me get a clip for your braid, get it up off your neck. Don't move, stay put." She turned and walked out, heading for the bathroom.

I looked at my sister. Her face was the colour of fresh beeswax. She watched the door Mom had gone through, her head craning forward as though to better hear the sound of retreating footsteps. The sound of a door opening was the signal for her chin to drop to her chest. From there, she slowly raised her eyes, looked straight at me, and said, in a low almost-whisper, "I'm scared."

I reached across the table and took her hand in mine. Her hand had none of the beeswax's warmth; it was cold and tense.

"I know," I said, and realized I did.

An animal can manage to limp along on three legs and find some semblance of balance again. But not on two. Faith just had to get better. Papi would have to look after himself.

XV

For two whole days Faith hadn't been out of bed without our help and then only for short trips to the bathroom for the usual reasons and for baths. She was no longer cold, she was burning up: the heat, a fever, the body's defence. Mom bathed her in the tub half-filled with water, cool water, plunging the sponge inside, ringing it out on each shoulder, water cascading down her back.

I didn't leave her side while she was in bed. I read her crosswords – I gave the clues, she gave the answers – plumped her pillows, brought her 7-up and ginger ale.

She turned to me as I bent over her, adding a third pillow under her head. "They won't find him you know."

I paused for a second, then pulled back as Faith settled against the pillows. "Wha…?"

"The hospital. They won't find Papi."

"How…?" Faith wasn't listening anymore. Not to me at least.

"Sometimes…" She looked down at her hands. "Sometimes I wonder whether he killed himself."

"Killed himself? What do you mean?"

"Papi. Do you think he would have? Taken his own life?" I came back into her sights.

"Why would you say that?"

"Because of the way he was those last weeks. So…"

"So…?"

"So quiet. So desperate. Searching everywhere. And now…"

"Now?"

"Now, well, it's like he's talking to me. From the other side."

I didn't even parrot her last remark.

"Talks isn't the right word. He communicates. That's it."

Another day, another time, Faith's hearing voices would have been a perfect opportunity to tease her, just the way she'd teased me about being a liver and a non-mammalian. But this was no joke.

"If it weren't for the… the talking, I'd think I was wrong. That he'd found what he was looking for. That he might be safely hidden away in a Buddhist monastery somewhere. Remember how he'd go on and on over dinner those last couple of months? All that stripping oneself of possessions and connections. Remember his meditation craze? That was when I learned yoga for the first time."

Another something I'd inherited from Papi. Ever since our trip to Xihuatanejo I'd started meditating. Okay, it was not really meditation. More like learning to hold my breath as long as I could. As long as my human limitations would let me, since it was impossible to regain the total freedom underwater the first mammals had known. If I just worked hard enough, I, like other free divers, could call up the ancient reflex that lets a whale divert blood and its oxygen from flippers or tails (in my case, arms and legs) to the heart and lungs. When I thought about it, really what I was trying to do might very well be the opposite of meditation, which was all *about* breathing if I remembered Papi correctly. I practised holding my breath in the hope that I'd have superhuman lung capacity the next time I went back to the ocean, enough to flip off my snorkel and free dive for as long as it took. Enough to never have to suffer from strangled lungs. The deeper a diver goes, the more air compresses; on the return, air expands. That was why scuba divers had to come up in stages to give the air time to circulate through their blood and empty, otherwise the veins could explode. In free diving, the quantity of air in the lungs stays the same, so as long as I learned to hold my breath, I could explore the depths and come back to the surface whenever it felt right.

"Remember that first day I got sick in the palace?" Just remembering brought back my own sick feeling of dread. "I was telling you about Nepautta, the in-between place. In-between the petrified lover volcanoes. Nepautta is where the poet Sor Juana was born. She was an amazing poet, but she stopped writing, very young, and retreated into convent life. Papi could have been the same. That's one way of stripping yourself of possessions and connections. A gentler way than suicide." She looked at me. To make sure I was listening, I thought. Then I realized it was to see how I would take what she had to say next. "But then he couldn't talk to me. So the other possibility is that he lost his life. Or took it. He didn't want to go crazy. He didn't want us to see him go crazy. Not again. That I know. And he wouldn't go back for treatment. It meant losing too much."

But if that was true, he could have trusted us enough to let us fight his demons by his side. He should have trusted us enough. We would have stood by him.

It was as though Faith had finally triggered my understanding of her earlier words. "He *talks* to you?"

"Well…," Faith hesitated. She was beginning to tire. It had been a long time since she'd spoken so much. "Just lately. Not talks really; he gives me signs."

"Signs?" I was back to my monosyllables. I couldn't seem to help myself.

"When I've needed him the most. This damn scirrhus. Sonnie. You know."

For the first time, I actually let the possibility that Papi might be dead enter my consciousness. But I realized even now, if Faith was right, my question hadn't changed, where was he? Where do they go, both the missing and the dead?

Faith seemed to be saying something else too, that, whether for monkdom or martyrdom, Papi left us to spare us. She, when her cancer (a word she never pronounced – scirrhus she called it instead, a word she plucked from her crossword book) had been discovered next to the foetus, had set herself on the same course, trying to spare her unborn child. Not monkdom or martyrdom, just protecting her nest.

I'd wanted to yell at Faith when I finally found out, which was only when the doctors insisted on seeing us and tracking down Papi to see if our stem cells might match hers. I wanted to ask her what the hell she thought she was doing, refusing treatment because of the slim chance her baby might be hurt. The doctors had said the chances the chemo treatment would be harmful to the foetus in the third trimester – radiation they did rule out – were not high. Your baby needs a mother, I wanted to cry. Look after yourself. That's how you can help your baby most. Look after yourself the way he should have done. But I said nothing then or now. Faith, despite her fatigue, hadn't finished.

"I never recognize the sign at the time. It's only after, once he's planted the seed. It's like the vehicle for his signs is in itself an expression of him. You know?"

A pause. Maybe. A bookstore, a poem, a picture sprung from poetry, a woman reclining, the shadows of the moon. The picture I'd begun to paint.

I wasn't sure, but I nodded anyway.

The December night we drove Faith to the hospital, our route was lined by crowds bearing candles. The nightly celebration of Las Posadas had begun. Nine nights to dramatize another journey in another time of another pregnant woman. We had to take Faith to the hospital because she couldn't keep anything down. Not even soft drinks or pills.

We called the doctor in the afternoon. He showed up two hours later. Some doctors actually made house calls in Mexico City. He was youngish, in his thirties, and as soon as I saw him I said to myself, he'll take care of Faith.

"I don't think we're going to be able to keep you at home any longer. You'll be needing glucose for the dehydration, and then… we'll see. At the hospital, you'll be under twenty-four-hour surveillance. We'll probably have to get more aggressive with the cancer now." Faith lifted her head to protest, but was too weak to speak.

I saw in him our saviour, someone not only to look after Faith's illness but to help bring up her child. I was labouring under a delusion. "Señorita, get real," would have been his reply. Nothing was real anymore.

"I suggest you get her things together. I'll call ahead to the hospital and have them prepare a room. Will you be able to transport her there soon?"

"Yes… yes, we will," I said.

Faith couldn't stand upright on our way to José's car. Her eyes couldn't seem to focus. She gave a little half-moan with every step. Once inside and moving, we watched the crowds illuminated by the wavering flicker of hundreds of tapers. The streets were overrun; any progress we made was at a pedestrian's pace. Faith's jagged breaths punctuated the murmurs and songs of the crowd.

Las Posadas. Mom sat cramped in the back with Faith's head in her lap, stroking her hair out of her eyes. I rolled my window down to try to get some air.

A small girl dressed as an angel led the crowd, children behind her carried two statues I couldn't see. Other children in silver and gold followed, then adults and musicians. The song's refrain kept echoing in my ears, a poignant plea for shelter. I rolled my window up.

XVI

The green picket fence again – pristine and headless this time – shimmered in the light then faded out of sight as another road opened up down which I turned. My feet moved underneath me as though on a moving sidewalk, my way traced out in advance. I came out into a clearing, and behind it saw a low pagoda-like building, the only sign of civilization. A tree bent in the breeze, its branches covered with millions of white shining ribbons. I clutched the paper covered with Papi's writing and stepped onto the porch.

The door knocker was in the shape of the Mexican eagle; its talons gripped the winged snake that formed the ring. I knocked. A man in a brown, hooded sackcloth answered. I gave him my father's name. Pedro Nebrija-Ruiz. Instead of giving me a blank look, he waved me inside, then held up his hand. He left me standing there.

This time I could hear my extra heartbeat, the one that is supposed to be innocent but felt quite lethal right then. Ja-ja, ja-ja, ja-ja-ja.

Two sets of footsteps sounded down the gallery to my left. The hallway was open to the outdoors, to a courtyard most likely, but the light flooding in blinded my eyes. Ja-ja, ja-ja, ja-ja-ja. I hugged myself with both arms to slow my heartbeat. When they stopped in front of me, I could finally see the second man. He was elderly, at least twenty years too old to be my father. I wanted to cry.

The old man stretched out his arm, pointed outside past where the light was flooding in. I walked out alone.

Stone benches surrounded a Zen garden: white sand, furrows, two large black rocks. A man with his back to me was at work in the centre of the garden. He held a hoe in his hands and was drawing it gently through the sand. His shoulders rose and fell while his body swayed like a pianist at the piano or a poet at his Selectric. The furrows he traced curved gracefully, silently.

From this angle I could see how each curve formed a letter, that together they made up a poem. I eased down onto the closest bench, my heart still pounding. My bag full of sketchpads and the old tin box in which I kept my charcoals clinked. The Zen gardener turned his head.

He laid down his rake, lifted up his robe, and stepped to the edge of the garden, making sure not to erase his masterpiece. It was only when his butterfly kiss touched my forehead – eyelash to skin – that I knew this man was Papi. By then it was too late. He was gone.

The clock read 3 a.m. I woke José up.

José held me, hushed me, but couldn't stop the tears. Finally he said, "This is what we will do. We'll go to Tepoztlán."

"When?" I sobbed.

"Now," he said.

I would flee the role of witness and find a way to intervene. Together we'd go to the pyramid and ask the gods to set things right.

The streets were eerie at this early morning hour, the deserted highway even more so.

We made the drive in silence. When I saw the turnoff for Tepoztlán, I remembered the picture in the paper the week before of the same sign and an abandoned car. The car a family had been driving before they stopped for the turnoff, perhaps on their way to the pyramid just like us. Bandits swarmed from the stunted bushes on the side of the road and threw open the back door to the car, demanding money. The father panicked and hit the gas pedal, but not before the bandit levelled his gun at the man's ten-year-old son sitting in the backseat and killed him instantly. Then the bandit fled.

Is cancer an evil that can be exorcised?

We parked on the edge of town and began the climb, José with his flashlight in hand. Outside its beam, nothingness. After the first bend in the path, I half expected to come across the same native women who'd been selling their trinkets when Faith and I attempted the hike so many eons ago. As if the women slept there at night.

I wished we had bought the silver charms on our way up. How could we have known that Faith would be too dizzy on our way back down? How could I have known we'd be needing them now?

I went up the ladder first, José behind me lighting the way. The shimmering beam, the climb, and my hands scraping against rock made me dizzy. At the top, I looked down to watch José follow, climbing awkwardly because of the flashlight in his right hand. Its beam swooped wildly through the night.

At the top of the mountain, we passed a deserted soft drink stand. Coca-Cola – It Purifies, it read. My muscles ached from the climb, my heart was straining, my breath came out in gasps. But I still asked, "Did you see that?"

José told me the Coca-Cola vendor carried all the glass bottles up on his back every day in a huge canvas bag strapped around his forehead. The miracle was that he could make it up.

We climbed the last few steps to the temple. Now only remnants of rooms were left and the ruin of an altar José said was used for offerings to the god. We climbed up stairs through twin pillars to the upper room. José pointed out an empty pedestal in the middle that used to bear the tablet with the figure of Tepoztecatl that the Spaniards smashed after the conquest because the natives refused to stop worshipping it.

The pyramid was tiny, not what I expected, but its size made the firmament seem more immense. The sun, as yet invisible, cast a soft glow on the sky. Only two stars and a sliver of moon could still be seen.

The sun was a god ascending, I was a speck on a planet whose orbit and angle had been decided in advance. The dawn, the breeze, the skies, the stones were all alive. I gave thanks.

Faith wasn't in her hospital room when I walked in bearing a bouquet of bright red anemones that I set by her bedside. I pulled the only chair up close and sat down. Maybe they'd taken her to Radiology for an ultrasound. Yes, that was it.

My hands played hopscotch on my knee, then Chinese skipping. Repeated the same motif over and over again. Ever since childhood, I'd traced the same pattern on my leg. I controlled the pattern. Maybe it controlled me. In any case, the repetition gave me peace.

This time I got no peace. I stood up, fidgety and anxious, and bent over to plump the pillow on Faith's bed. I felt something hard underneath. Lifted the pillow. Saw my sketchbook. The one I'd left here just in case. Just in case I had the time or the will to draw Faith. Why was it under her pillow? I opened it up, saw not sketches but pages of doodling. Mine. That's right, I'd scribbled instead, my mind empty of images, any connection had been cut with my hand. The alphabet written over and over like a text that never ended. A circle that spiralled out from itself, round and round, bigger and bigger. Pressure building as inevitably as the circle spiralled. As Faith's body was breaking down, so did everything remotely linked to her. Even the boom box quit working the day Faith was admitted to hospital. I tried everything to get it going again. The nurses let me borrow a needle, even a scalpel to pick at its inner workings. It remained mute.

I took Faith's watch home the night she was admitted to make sure it wouldn't get stolen. But now it kept stopping every hour or two, except when it worked like a charm. If only it were a charm. Today on my walk from the metro to the hospital, I saw a sparrow plummet from the branches of a tree and die at my feet. Involuntarily, I stopped breathing, afraid of the inodorous fumes both the sparrow and I had shared.

My doodles weren't the only markings. Faith had made my sketchbook hers.

(Key of D)
C: Without the aid of speech or of sight
My mother's granddaughter taught me a language
More potent than the strongest drug
I speak my daughter tongue.

The other drugs they offer me
I refuse, they'd hinder our talk
And hamper my awkward fumbling
In the language she's invented for us

C: Without the aid of speech or of sight
My mother's granddaughter taught me a language
More potent than the strongest drug
I speak my daughter tongue.

A language of finger touch and fluttering
Words for hunger and thirst and for love
A language I have not chosen
A language reserved for us

C: Without the aid of speech or of sight
My mother's granddaughter taught me a language
More potent than the strongest drug
I speak my daughter tongue. A language of love.

Under the neatly printed song were nine words, scrawled
in sprawling letters across the bottom of the page. *Hope*, I
read, *please. This and all the others for Sonnie.* I was deathly
afraid.

I heard footsteps in the hall and dropped the sketchbook
on the bed. The doctor walked in, his face a mask.

In my mind I drew babies, not knowing the impossibility of
the task. I didn't know the way a baby's features are still
unformed once she makes her entrance into the world, how
they would only take on line, detail, and shape over the coming days, like a ship emerging from the fog. I was like an
Aztec artist at the time of the Conquest painting imagined
European women in Western finery, dark strong faces and
chiselled noses, transposing the known onto the unknown.

When Sonnie was born, I should have been there to
record this emergence and capture every finest point on
paper for her to see when she was old enough to understand.
But I could only draw from an imagining, make a record to
which I would return.

It was José who told me of the blurred perfection of Sonnie's newborn features. I wouldn't know. I stayed on the other side of the Cesarean screen with my mother, one of us on either side of Faith, staring at the mask on her face, at the stray hairs from her ponytail trapped inside, the machine by the bed, her eyelids held closed by a thin strip of tape that barely fluttered as instruments clanged against bowls. I didn't see crimson blood gush over scalpeled skin folds, Sonnie bubble up, rivulets flow, or spent placenta oozing, giver of life.

When the baby was born shortly after midnight on December 21st, they whisked her into the hall from where José watched while my mother and I kept vigil at Faith's side.

Sonnie was fuzzy perfection, he said, not bright red or wrinkled or deformed. Perfection waiting to unfurl.

Sonnie was born perfection.

But then her mother died.

XVII

Todo madre. In Spanish todo madre means everything's fine. All mother. Everything's fine.

When a mother dies before she sees her child, there is no todo madre. When that mother's mother watches her first-born die…

God can only be a He. A She could never stand back and do nothing. A She wouldn't disappear when you needed Her most.

They said the baby was in danger. That they had to go in and get her then and there. So they put Faith under. But she never came up again.

I lost my sister that day. I lost my mother, too. My father was already gone.

I will tell it like it is. I will tell of the surgeon, how he came and kneeled at my mother's side as they wheeled Faith from the operating room. I will tell of his eyes, full of the pain a father might feel on losing a child. I will tell how my mother asked, "Is she going to die?" And of his answer – yes.

I should have reached for Mom then and her for me, if all the lines we'd been fed were true: tragedy draws the stricken together, prayers will be answered, God never sends more than a body can bear. But they weren't, and we didn't. I knew I should have comforted her. I knew she should have comforted me. But we were locked in separate worlds, alternate worlds. The surgeon went off into his. He deserted us there, but gave us his cell phone first. To call the baby's father he said. My mother whispered, "Kiko, call Kiko," and I obeyed.

I had to go outside, no cell calls allowed in a hospital room. I could no longer stand. My spine had collapsed and no longer knew which way was up. The retaining wall at my back retaining me, not the plants behind. The night sky, Mom, José huddled round me. My head bowed to my knees, I made the call to tell my sister's lover, forced each syllable out. Left a message.

Tiny, white cuff of black coif riding down on her forehead, little sparrow hands raised to touch my cheek, smile of sympathy on her face, she accosted me. At the door into Intensive Care, Sor Rosario brought her hands down to mine, held my gaze, said, you will see, how beautiful it is.

I jerked my hands away, raised them high as if to ward her off. As if to form a cross. It worked for vampires, didn't it? I muttered, a mistake, the shock, we didn't ask for you, our friend will come. Thinking, you don't know us, you don't know Faith, take your pity, your salvation and go home. She left.

Mom waved me feebly inside the ICU, the unit for intensive care. My turn with Faith.

I had never known what it was to be touched by grace. Faith gave me that.

She was there, still alive, flesh hot to the fingertips. Flesh I had touched so many times. I could hold her and kiss her cheeks, her forehead, again and again. Over and over find comfort in her breath, even distorted by the mask. Minutes I was given that I will never have again. Seconds not minutes, each more important than the last. The wonder of being allowed to say goodbye. I never said goodbye to Papi. To her I said farewell.

I held her hand, touched her belly, laid my head on her chest. Stroked the soft down on her arms, so abundant she called it her curse. A curse. A curse.

The sound of a door opening shattered the seconds I had left. I looked up. Saw José. His face was white, his neck had disappeared. I turned to Faith.

He put a hand around my waist, touched Faith's face. He stood, I sat. José clasped his hands around hers, turned over first the left, then the right. I saw her lifeline, the way it petered out.

"I told her to stay," he whispered. At first, I thought he meant Faith. He'd gone mad. Then it came to me, no, he meant the nun. "The doctor told me now. If we want. For last rites." A pause. "She's out there with your mother." I looked at Faith, tried to comprehend that in short minutes, the number of seconds finite, she had lost her baby, and soon would lose her life. I nodded.

They filed in together, Sor Rosario and Mom. The lights were dim, the nun's voice still now, steady, saying, Verás lo bello que es.

We sat together, two on either side of Faith – my mother, José, Sor Rosario and I – our hands clasped on Faith's still rising falling chest. The steel clamp on her index finger glowed red as did her flesh. The ventilator whooshed in, whooshed out. We read from the sparrow nun's vellum book, sang in muted, trembling tones, voices joined, tears travelling our cheeks. He became a She for me and spoke in a rush of air through my chest, in a tingling of follicles along my scalp. I had never known such beauty to exist.

Grace only lasts for an instant; that instant had to last me a lifetime. After Grace comes Fury, a daughter of Earth and of Night. Centuries later, I stumbled from the hospital to the metro, my mother – joined by Kiko – refusing to leave her dead daughter's side. I had murder in my heart, thoughts of empty wombs, ghosts of fathers, and corpses, ashen, frozen and forsaken. José was at my side, unseen, unheard, invisible in my fog.

The stench of metro filled my open pores, abrased my skin, drained fury from my limbs. In the near-empty car, doors glided on air while I slumped at the window, eyes closed, breath expelled. Nothing. I pried open muscles, tendons, jaw, cerebral stem to leave a gap, a wound, a space for her to enter in. No one. I spoke her name. Never again.

Up subway steps, down. Narrow streets. I hung from the railing as I climbed the outer stairs, scraped up each step, watched slivers stud my knees. Wrenched open the door, crawled to a chair.

José walked past, hesitated, then walked over to the phone. Flicker of red blinking, message light on Faith's answering machine. Press. Rewind. "We're not in," her voice said. "Call us some other time." José groaned into tears.

I dragged my body up like a wreck from the seabed. Crossed the room, put my arms on José's shoulders, my head against his back as it shook.

He cradled my arms wrapped around him, head down.

Blare of music, mist of voice singing low, indecipherable. I pressed Rewind.

Individual notes rang out, lyrics still unheard. Pressed again. Rewind. Irridescent sound. "Believe in me/I hear your voice."

Veins like seaweed bulbs burst, flooding my empty womb with ocean spray.

XVIII

When Sonnie was old enough to listen, what would I say? Before anything, I'd tell her of her mother. But my version of my sister's life would be as unreliable, as flawed, as aching with love and loss as I. As unreliable and flawed and aching as my love had been.

For now, Sonnie wasn't old enough to listen. Sonnie didn't know she had lost her mother. I was the mother she saw.

Me, a mother. Become a mother in an instant. In a santiamén, the Spanish word for instant. José called me Saint Amen. Amen meaning this is true, yes, and so be it. Amen was another word for God.

My sister was dead, and I was alive. I'd found a place where guilt had meaning, where we could go, my guilt and I, confess and be absolved.

I'd found a place to go when the hatred got too much. Hatred of the doctors, the invisible killers, my mother for giving up, myself. Hatred, I'd discovered, was a slow death. Mexico's volcanoes – the couple of legend – began as towers of rage at the injustice of death stripping them of love. I could see Mom's features taking on the rigidity of the now sleeping volcanoes. I refused to be cast in stone. I wanted to live.

I'd found the opposite of hate; a place that embraced all beings. José told me I might be going overboard. It's better than going under I said.

The opposite of hate offered the here and the after. The hereafter. My niece's grandfather had walked this path before me, in my dreams at least, he just chose another branch. Buddhist over Catholic. His enlightened being to my Christ.

I got religion because it beat the alternative. I got religion just like him. I was my Papi's girl.

I am become the daughter, helpless, lost. My dove, my love, my life. How can I go on without you?

I am become the daughter, you the guide.

Mom's writing. She offered only this. Faith's journal – Mom's journal now – lay beside the bed. Mom's bed now in the maid's room on the roof, its paneless window and empty door frame open to the stars, the moon, and the dark. Night and day, day and night, I spent with the baby in the Cuernavaca apartment, what used to be Mom's place. José came to us on weekends. Since the funeral.

Faith's funeral held in a room off the morgue of the American hospital, led by a chaplain I had never seen, before or since. If only Sor Rosario had led the service – but then it would be called a mass – with her bright eyes, papery hands, and raised veins that throbbed like wings. If only I could have listened to her words again, "Verás lo bello que es."

The minister wore a suit, a business suit for a man of trade. His clerical collar was grey from overuse and shiny from wear. He stood at the head of the coffin; we the mourners, ten in all – Mom, Graciela and Miguel, Anouk, Alan, Claude, Kiko, José, and Sonnie – at the foot. He didn't sing; he droned. That was when Sonnie began to wail, and I walked out.

Every second or third gulp, she jerked away from the bottle to give a weak cry. Four ounces of milk didn't last nearly long enough. We got back before he finished, saw him wave the mourners forward, say take your time with your goodbyes. How much time did he think we would need? Mom didn't budge, nor did anyone else. So I hitched Sonnie to my shoulder, marched up, past the body they said was my sister, past the man in a suit, and into the hall.

Leonardo da Vinci dissected corpses. Not for his art, the way people thought, not to learn the body, its muscles, nerves, and flesh. He was looking for the soul. He wasted his time. I could tell my sister's soul had long departed her shell.

The minister didn't have the decency to close the doors. We huddled in the corridor next to a fake Christmas tree, under a piñata; no one told us what came next. Not him, not the two morgue workers who carried the coffin lid past us to where her body lay, then glued the coffin tight before our gaze. Sharp fumes wafted through that open door, pricked my nostrils, stung my eyes. My body convulsed.

In my arms, Sonnie wailed. My mother stood like a woman who had been robbed of her senses, unable to hear, see, smell, or feel. Mothers are as fragile as civilization, someone once said. I waited for the world to end.

I didn't want to leave our apartment in Mexico City. Our nest. I didn't want to leave Faith's bathtub, and the soap on the ledge. I didn't want to leave the fridge, the guayaba, the baby bananas and papaya we bought for her. The fruit was ripe for eating, but Faith wasn't alive. I didn't want to leave our closet and her huaraches still so new you couldn't see the imprint of her foot. I didn't want to leave. I wanted her to know she could always come back.

My mother said one thing, one thing only. When only one thing is said, it is meant to be heard. "Twenty-two-million people live in Mexico City, but my daughter died here. Her daughter won't."

Kiko was the last person to say goodbye to us in the city. He knocked as I was on my knees in front of the bathroom sink, sliding the plastic bag and its sheaf of looseleaf papers from its hiding place. It was in my hand as I opened the door. Outside, helicopters droned, demonstrators filled the streets, white balloons floated between the humans on the ground and the mechanical dragonflies in the sky. Soldiers above and below cradled rifles in their arms. Manifestación, Chiapas, TLC. His words came back to me as told to me by Faith. "When violence has been done to you, violence grows in your heart."

Kiko's slender hands trembled slightly as he held out a potted poinsettia. He raised a hand and tucked his hair behind his ear. "The flower, it's for women in childbirth," he said. He swallowed, "Who die…" His eyes filled with tears. He took a breath. "Those women come back… for its nectar," he pointed at the plant. Sonnie cried out behind me. He followed me inside, bent over her lying between pillows on our bed – now mine alone – and put his hand next to her fist. Her fingers opened and grasped his baby finger. She brought the finger to her mouth.

I had never before seen tears bounce in the shape of perfect pearls from a man's lashes to his cheeks.

I must find out if Faith's all right.

I wanted to cry out, "Of course she isn't, she's dead!" but I knew better. A mother doesn't stop being a mother just because her child has died.

But this mother had a grandchild. She should be asking whether her granddaughter was all right. She didn't. Because acknowledging Sonnie's existence meant acknowledging too much?

Why didn't she ask whether I was all right? Because I wasn't.

Life is a gift I've accepted, exclaimed over, and only rarely, just recently, wanted to give back.

Time slowed, and the outside world fell away in the huddle of grief. Nothing had changed, everything had changed, how could that be?

All I had was the present, these rooms, this crib. Tomorrow was never guaranteed. But the present was too much. Sonnie rarely slept, my mother never spoke, the present was too hard to take in, too painful to hold, but I did. I held it tight and long.

XIX

I'd gone to the roof to look for the ironing board. The journal was lying on Mom's bed. I hadn't searched it out.

I picked it up out of habit, opened it. That first entry jumped out at me. The shock – Faith's come back! – then the reality. The handwriting this time Mom's.

I hadn't searched it out for days. But that last entry haunted me. *Life is a gift I've accepted, exclaimed over, and only rarely, just recently, wanted to give back.* I didn't understand her words. I didn't want to give my life back. I just wished Faith could be given hers.

What if Mom did give her life back? The thought chased my sorrow with fear and a need to prevent. Knowledge was the only defence I had. But Mom stayed in her room almost all the time, slept during the day, sat outside to watch the stars at night. Finally on the weekend when José came back, he offered to make her a window box for Kiko's poinsettia – nochebuena was the name he used for it – and bird feeders to feed all her birds. She went down to the workshop, my studio, to show him what she wanted. I could slip into her room unseen.

I read that before we are born, we choose the people we love, the way we live, the time we die. You chose us.

I never knew being one of the chosen could hurt so much.

Whatever I write, Faith, and I must write because I can't speak, you must never think I wish you hadn't chosen me, chosen us. I promise you, here, today, tomorrow and every day to come, that the anguish at having lost you will never, ever be greater than the gift of having had you. I promise you that.

The family I thought I'd created is crumbling away, my fear is it will soon be nothing but ripples on the sand. We will return to the time before, to the beginning. "In the beginning… the earth was a formless wasteland and darkness covered the abyss." The Bible's beginning. The beginning Hope believes in. That I cannot. The Bible says God took just seven days to create the universe. That universe, its seven days like the seven prongs of a piñata, was destroyed with one swing of the stick.

All the certainties that come from living forty-seven years in one body have been shed. I lost the man I loved, and the daughter I birthed. In my dreams, she's still alive. She is 2, she is 4, she's a teen, she's a woman, and each time I have to tell her she's dying. Awake I live in fear of losing the others.

The mother tongue I taught my daughters was a lie, a silencing. In it, I taught that life was good, and just, and patient, and kind. To do that, I had to deny so much. Pedro, madness, injustice. The hurt. I need another tongue. One that says that life can be unspeakably cruel and unfair. And as beautiful as the night sky. That life can drain from a woman giving birth while infecting her newborn with its force. That is the only language I can speak. Not the mother tongue I taught.

I felt unclean when I closed the pages. But I said to myself, sometimes you have to get dirty to stay clean. To stay free of the stain of future guilt and to prevent what might have come.

I wished a painting could be made for every pregnant woman who had died, for every life that could have been, for every life that was. But I wasn't ready yet.

I wished a painting could be made for every woman who had lost a child. But I wasn't ready yet.

They say a newborn baby sees life, her surroundings, as a series of paintings. Not yet understanding how one painting leads to the next.

I missed the smell of oils and wax and fresh wood and turpentine. I missed the feel of a virgin canvas under my hand. I missed its transformation, the layers growing, the colours glowing. I missed my sketchbook, now beside my mother's bed. I missed not having any pictures to transmit. Everything I missed rushed back when Anouk came to call.

She stood at the door, a big cardboard box in her hands, the whiff of turpentine in her hair. I kissed her cheek, she mine. I motioned her to a chair and searched for something to say. She pointed to the box.

On top, a half-dozen baby bottles and nipples. On the bottom baby clothes. Long dresses and jumpers in dark colours, white cotton diaper toppers, and undershirts. In a tiny shoe box, a pair of brown huaraches.

"They're hand-me-downs, but…"

I started to cry. Anouk stood, reached over, and pulled me into her arms. I was in the embrace of a woman's body again, no jutting bones or hard muscle but gentle roundness and comfort.

When Anouk left, neither of us knew when she'd be back. I understood now how difficult it could be, she the mother of a toddler back in the city too many kilometres away.

Alone again. Another day until José got back, until the weekend. So much changed in such a short time. Faith, Sonnie, my mother, and José. His "for now" become so permanent. He had adopted us or we him. Sonnie he called his *chiquitita*, not just *chica*, girl, or *chiquita*, honey, but *chiquitita*, the tenderest endearment there was. My time with her he didn't resent. For my mother, he was not quite as understanding, his

silences asking why did she have to be added to my list.
Losing Faith had yet to teach him that. But he knew I was
here to stay, and so was he. I who had thought short months
ago that one-night stands were all I would ever know.

But for now, alone again. Time to myself, Sonnie asleep,
time to relive again and again the past. Sonnie's name in
Spanish came out Sony. José said her name matched her
stereo set of lungs. She could cry. And did, often at night in
Dolby stereo. Leaving no room for thought. That was good.

I used to try to ward off her tears by anticipating her
every want, but I soon realized that babies have a need to cry.
All I could do was hold her while she wept.

When I moved down from the city, José moved my studio gear into the only garage in the Cuernavaca compound, Miguel and Graciela's garage. They insisted, saying
they'd park in the driveway with the other tenants. The cars
had to be parked one behind the other there, and the car
owners had to agree on who would park where. The last car
in line was the first to leave in the morning, otherwise no
one else could get out. All that trouble, and I hadn't even
set foot in the new studio. That was how José got himself a
workshop.

Another night, another dream. I dreamt I could draw again.
Papi and his Zen garden on a canvas in the shape of an hourglass. The knobs to the secret doors were so small they
looked like little more than grains of sand. The hourglass was
empty. From a hole at the bottom, sand gushed out like water
from a fountain. Sand so white it looked like snow. Snow so
white it was blue.

The trick was to keep moving, keep busy, keep patrolling our new space. I would care for my sister's daughter, and be there to help define for her the boundaries of our patch of coral reef. Not for me a swim off into open waters never to look back, letting fate and the currents do the rest.

I read the newspaper to Sonnie every morning. She'd know her past before her ABC's. As did every Mexican. Every Sunday at five o'clock every radio station throughout the country played the same history program. The first time I sat switching stations, I thought all radios in Mexico played the same program all day long.

The daily cry of the tamales peddlar passing down our street – Tamales! Tamales! – was another part of her history. As was the Spanish language, a language in which death translated as a passing state, not a finality. In Spanish Sonnie's mother's identity wasn't defined by her death; it wasn't a curt "Faith es muerta" but a softer, gentler "está muerta." This too shall pass.

I took her on the bus – the ruta – down, down past three traffic circles, glorietas, until we were so close to downtown we were better off walking alongside the bus through streets jammed with traffic, pedestrians, and vendors. So much to see, to smell, to hear, to taste. We would do it all. Everything Faith had never had the chance to discover, we would.

I lifted Sonnie out of the old tin basin I used to bathe her in, a hand under each armpit to get a proper grip, and wrapped her in a terry towel then flipped up the terry hood. She squirmed without wriggling free. With her in the crook of one arm, I grabbed her bottle from the warm water in the sink.

Three weeks old now. Her eyes never left my face as she nursed. With her short arms, she tried to grab my nose, the dust motes, a ray of light. Instead she grabbed my breast through my shirt, then turned to look at the bunched-up fabric clutched tight in her fist. Her eyes swivelled back to mine saying, did you see what I got.

When I pulled away the empty bottle, her lips kept moving just in case. I gave her a kiss, inhaled baby talcum, used the words she could echo back. Ajá, ajá. So much better than goo-goo-ga. So different from the night's routine when she dozed as the bottle emptied, woke up with a start to continue, then dropped off again, her mouth working so feebly on the nipple that the milk stayed trapped inside.

I dressed her in rompers from Anouk's box, slipped both arms into the Snugli, tightened the belt around my hips, slid Sonnie inside, and did up the snaps. She arced back, left, then right, sensing the amount of space, then settled in. Faith had spent hours poring over the L.L. Bean catalogue, deciding whether to buy a Snugli or a kiddies backpack, then splurged and ordered both.

They came the day after her funeral as I was packing to move. A delivery boy knocked at the door, asked for Faith. I signed.

Instead of taking the street that led to the ruta, I veered left to search out a park.

I walked past a newsstand and the woman attendant talking to a customer out front. As I passed the side door to the tiny stall, I saw a foot sticking out. The small boy inside lay stretched out on a mat. He could have been anywhere from two to five years old. Size meant nothing down here. His eyes stared out at me, then turned to the baby. He didn't wave or smile. I felt like stretching out my hand and taking him with us to play in a playground or run in the grass.

I did find a park, one without trees or grass, but most of all I found a church. I saw the woman first.

I saw her from the back, sitting on a bench at the foot of the churchsteps. When the bells began to chime, she pushed slowly off the bench, tipped forward at a dangerous angle, straightened her knees, and then her back. She was old, thin as a stickman or a tiny bird.

Sor Rosario. I hurried forward to catch her as she went up the steps. Then she turned and looked back. The lines on her forehead and either side of her mouth were like tracks dug in wax. Every inch of her skin was feathered with creases, but she had no veins like wings.

I forgot about Sor Rosario for an instant, saw old age as if for the first time. How did a person get to be old? This woman, so frail, how had she survived? What was her secret?

Other people brushed past me on their way into the church. Old people with hunched shoulders who favoured their hips. I followed them inside.

The first old woman made her way halfway down the centre aisle, where she bent on one knee, genuflected, then slid into a pew. I sat right behind her, unzipped the Snugli, pulled Sonnie out, and turned her around. Sonnie reached out to try to catch a wisp of white hair. Her hands came up empty.

The woman leaned on the back of the pew in front of her, eased one knee then the other down on the kneeling bench, and rocked back slightly on her feet.

All around me the others were doing the same. Once on their knees, no one clasped their hands, most kept open eyes. Some half-sat on the pew, one knee on the kneeler, their backs too bad to go all the way down. They knelt in the quiet of the sanctuary and didn't make a show of prayer. No one wore their Sunday best; this mass was a part of their day, like going for bread.

The woman ahead of me struggled to her feet. Only then did I see the priest walking down the aisle. As he drew closer to the front, the scattered rows ahead stood up, creating a miniature wave like at a hockey game. Or more like a ripple. I wondered if the ripple reversed as the priest left after mass.

The priest spoke, the people responded. Fifty voices – less mine – all speaking as one. We rose together, we sat

together, we knelt at the same time. We sang in unison, unac-
companied, the beauty of fifty voices where a choir has only
one.

At one point, the priest chanted. Such a beautiful, haunt-
ing sound. I had never heard anyone chant before.

On an unspoken cue, the first row of worshippers
stepped out in the aisle and began to move to the front. The
second row followed, then the third, each row waiting for the
last person in the row ahead before stepping out into the
aisle. All moved forward slowly with shuffling feet and hands
clasped in front. The row ahead of mine started out, I pushed
back in my seat to let my row pass then watched them make
their way down the aisle: fat, thin, limping, grizzled. There
was beauty again.

I didn't see the ripple at the end of mass. I was crying, for
Faith, for Papi, for my mother, for myself.

XX

It was Friday, the day Sonnie turned one month old. She was in her crib asleep, and I was waiting for José.

Waiting was never something I did well. There was always the chance the person I was waiting for would never show up. I was a pacer, a too-rattled-to-read thinker, and a stewer when I had to wait. I tiptoed out the front door.

Nights are pitch dark in Cuernavaca. The dark made me shiver, even in the heat. I liked my darkness tempered by light, by street lamps, and a city glow. In this dark of absolutes, the few metres between our building and Mom's seemed like an ocean too deep to cross.

I looked toward the maid's room and heard a low, repeated whistle – Mom's. I walked over to my bedroom window, peeked in on Sonnie, who hadn't budged from where I'd laid her down, curled up on her stomach, her knees gathered under her, her rear end stuck in the air. Sleeping the sleep of the just. Maybe Faith had known better than me. In an ice age, a mother's womb can serve as a barrier against acid rain, but in our day it offers no protection against chemicals injected by human hands.

The window was open and the screen up to keep mosquitoes out. I'd only be gone for a minute or two, if she cried I'd hear her from the roof. Sound rises; the higher you are the closer you are to the ground.

As I passed in front of the landlords' open door, Graciela
stepped out on the stoop. "Hola, Esperanza."

Graciela lost her son fifteen years ago. Fifteen years and
he still had his altar and his name on people's lips. From the
outside, people looked so whole. I realized now that all
wholeness was made up of jagged, torn, and missing pieces.

Graciela and Miguel told my mother not to worry about
getting back to work, to give herself time, she could start
back slowly doing administrative tasks and only teach when
she felt ready.

On the ironing table in her bedroom, I'd seen the school
correspondence and brochures my mother was working on.
It seemed such a shame to render into proper English
Miguel's correspondence to prospective students and lose all
the effusive exuberance, but to English ears it would only
sound insincere. *En su fax me manifiesta sus deseos de asistir a
nuestros cursos intensivos de español; mismos que hemos venido
impartiendo desde hace 24 años ININTERRUMPIDAMENTE,
por lo que puede tener la SEGURIDAD Sr., que obtenga una
buena capacitación del español y una estancia ¡MUY PLACEN-
TERA! entre todos nosotros. Deseo de todo corazón que encuentre
el ¡EXITO! tanto en su vida privada como en nuestro curso.
Atentamente: Su NUEVO AMIGO que lo estima: Miguel Villa,
Director General.* The double exclamation marks, the capital
letters, the undying promises of friendship and affection
would all have to go. I was suddenly glad to be living in a
country and a language that knew nothing of holding back.

Miguel's letter *was* sincere. Just as Miguel's and Graciela's
offer of the rooftop room rent-free was sincere. And conven-
ient – it was no use to them now since an electric dishwasher
had replaced their maid.

My mother must have heard the two of us because she'd
fallen silent by the time I stepped onto the roof. She was on
her one and only chair outside watching the stars through
her binoculars. Kiko's binoculars. The ones he'd left for her

on his first trip down. I hadn't realized when Faith was alive just how close she and Kiko had grown. Kiko now told a side of my sister as yet unknown. Told my mother, though, not me. Because in Kiko's eyes, once religion reared its head, I went from friend to foe.

There were stars, thousands of them. The ground was dark, but the sky was pricked through with lights.

I grabbed the ironing stool from Mom's room and set it down beside her. We still hadn't spoken a word.

José said 90 percent of new discoveries in the firmament are made by amateur astronomers. Maybe Mom would find something new out there. That was what I told myself. She, however, didn't need a reason for gazing, gazing was reason enough. I wanted her to have some purpose. Kiko didn't ask her for anything, just gave her what she needed to look.

She lowered the binoculars and motioned for me to have a turn. She pointed above our heads. Mom did speak now. Just not often and not much. "Over there, like a necklace." I brought the binoculars to my face. "Orion – Kiko calls it Hotumkono – strung together like beads on a string." It took my eyes a minute to focus. She was right. Like a necklace, or a rosary. "Just below it, see, in that cloud of gas and dust, new stars are forming."

The stars transported me back to our apartment in Mexico City, to our bedroom, and our pasted ceiling constellations. These stars were so alive, winking and blinking, growing stronger then weaker then stronger again. The stars in our bedroom never changed. Maybe that was why I'd given up on art, I now knew it was impossible to capture life on paper, spray it with fixative, and trust it would never change.

Perched on the stool, I could see the top of Mom's head and the swirl of a snow-white patch near the back of her skull, a patch that never used to be there. She had shrunk since Faith's death. She who'd been known to catch and crush a wasp in her bare hand without flinching to get Faith and me to stop squealing now put a limp hand in mine. With Faith gone, I'd lost the only other person who could understand the difficulties of daughtering this particular mother. Another loss. Daughtering. An art unto itself.

She pointed above us. Her voice was soft. "That's her star, there. The brightest. Sirius." I looked.

Maybe that was why Faith called her cancer scirrhus. By giving her illness another name, she thought she could make it an ally instead of a foe.

I heard the thud of the latch at the iron gate, the creak as it swung back, and the crunch of gravel as a car drove down the slope. José.

Mom spoke before I could call out. "You go on down. I'll stay put." Her voice was flat again, lifeless.

As I put the stool back, I knocked over the urn at the foot of Mom's bed. Ashes spilled onto the floor. I gathered them up in my hands, stoppered the lid, and backed out the door.

José and I tried making love that night for the first time since Faith died. But I had to stop halfway, crying tears of sand.

XXI

José went with us to mass on Sunday. As a favour to me. His
church-going usually limited to major holidays or special
petitions – I remembered Guadelupe – because of a mother-
imposed drill when he was a child. Being dragged to daily
mass and forced to say Hail Marys on his knees morning and
night for all those years had turned him off practising. But it
hadn't drummed out his faith. His mother. A woman I might
just never meet. Unless her terms were met: a proper conversion and wedding to make things look right. José didn't have
much patience for hypocrisy. But he believed in family ties.

This time I actually listened to the homily instead of sim-
ply letting myself be rocked by the music of the words. The
priest's voice boomed in the vaulted church. "There is something incongruous about the image of the shepherd and his
sheep. Sheep aren't very bright. They have to be herded. They
give nothing back. I think the image of wild horses best
describes man's relationship with God. A creature who needs
taming. Once tamed, a horse learns to recognize love and
gives love in return. A horse has to be broken to be tamed.
The same holds true for us. Only when we are broken do we
discover God."

Broken.

The joined voices for the hymn we sang, *Shepherd me, O
God, beyond my wants, beyond my fears, from death into life,*

brought tears back to my eyes, the Amen and the Hosannah
sent shivers of hope down my scalp. Words registered with
me this time, not just the ritual sound.

Thanks to José I learned that I too, the non-Catholic,
could walk up the aisle with the others when the time came,
all I had to do was cross my arms on my chest for a blessing
instead of reaching out for the host. Gently, the priest laid his
hand on my forehead. Under the palm of his hand, my
mind's eye sprang to life.

The words I'd mouthed with the others before the journey down the aisle came back to me, "Lord I am not worthy
to receive you, but only say the words and I shall be…
healed." Healed. That last word so unexpected, so unneces-
sary, so right.

A step to foster healing – Mom's and mine – came to me the
next morning with the first light. Two steps. One I could do
something about right away. The other would take some time.

José had to be up at five to leave for the city. I got up
with him. I followed him out to the driveway and watched
him back the car up the hill then turned to the garage meant
for my studio.

Boxes of canvases and paints and my hobbyhorse easel
were all pushed back into the corner where they'd been left
when we moved them in. They would be part of step two.
For now, I tugged and pulled each one out of the way, feeling my muscles protest as I did. The hammock – step one –
was lying on the floor at the very back.

I slung the hammock over my arm, dropped a hammer,
a box of nails, and a wrench in the sling, and made my way
over to the ladder. Everything was quiet on the rooftop.

Mom's chair still sat outside the door. Her chair with its
straight back that obliged her to crane her neck back as far

as it would go to see her beloved stars. This was something I could do for her. Better than shovelling snow once your loved one had already left.

It turned out I didn't need either the hammer or the wrench, which meant I wouldn't disturb Mom's sleep. All I needed was almost forgotten knot-tying skills – finally I had something to show for my brief but boring stint in a Girl Guide company.

At regular intervals along the flat rooftop, bare metal rods stuck straight out, some with another horizontal bar attached like crosses. In Mexico property owners often left buildings partially unfinished to avoid paying property tax.

I was able to attach the hammock to a metal cross on either side of the roof using a reef knot. I leaned all my weight onto my fists to test it out. The rough jute cord left a diamond pattern on my knuckles. I sat down. The wooden bars at each end through which the cord ran creaked as I settled in, but the knots looked sturdy enough to hold. I lay back. The last time I'd slept in the hammock was with Faith – alive – in the bed at my side.

Teardrops pooled in the hollow of my neck, a salt pool. Salt of longing. I fell asleep.

Sonnie's cooing woke me. In her second month, she'd become so much more vocal, more awake. Her stroller was positioned next to my head. Mom must have brought her up from downstairs. Through the doorway, I could see Mom lift a battered pot off the Coleman stove. The sweet smell of hierbabuena wafted out to me.

I held out my finger, cleansed of all salt. Sonnie grabbed it with both hands and suckled.

Mom set the tray on the ground and sat on her chair. I leaned over, the hammock tipping with me, to pick up my tea and roll back, the cup balanced on my chest. Sonnie, meanwhile, had found the end of the strap to her stroller and had transferred her gums to it.

When we'd both had time to let the mint and molten sugar open up our throats and warm our vocal chords, Mom spoke first. "Thank you for the hammock."

I waved my hand vaguely, "For stargazing."

"I know," Mom said.

Another silence broken only by Sonnie milking her strap.

"You wouldn't think she'd had her bottle."

"Hmmm."

Then out of nowhere, "Crying helps."

Involuntarily, my hand went to my lips. My body was constantly giving away my secrets. For hours after I cried, the skin above my lip stayed patchy red as did my nose, and my eyes looked permanantly bloodshot. There was nothing I could say.

Back in the studio later that day, searching through all the boxes of finished paintings and unfinished canvases, I came across the picture sprung from a poem, started but never finished. Seeing the woman on canvas instead of in my mind, she no longer looked asleep. She looked like she had died.

Several frames behind it lay the 3D canvas José made for me a lifetime ago. I stood and stared. But for the first time in a long time, I wanted to do more than look.

I knew I had no choice anyway but to go back to my art. If only for the money from my grant. Especially now that it looked like José's application to the regional government to start up a school program in the Cuernavaca market was going to be approved. I'd need the grant and then another job. We might want a bigger apartment if he was able to move here, one with a separate room for Sonnie. But I'd told José we'd have to wait until one of the other tenants in my building left. I wouldn't move from here. I wouldn't leave my mother. She was all I had left of the past. Mom wouldn't leave her rooftop perch. A perch it was. Every day she filled the bird feeder José made for her. Chickadees, sparrows, and finches trilled through the yard and up to the roof where they hovered, waiting their turn. And hummingbirds sipped from the poinsettia. Birds by day, the stars by night.

I'd taken to sitting by the unused pool out front on the nights I was in Cuernavaca on my own. By the pool that Graciela kept promising would warm up enough come summer for us to be able to brave a swim. Four strong strokes, five at most, would take me from one side of the kidney-shaped basin to the other. I wouldn't count on it for my daily exercise.

I did count on it for some peace of mind. Even if it was a sorry substitute for the ocean, the gentle ripples and chirping of palm leaves brought on by the night breeze helped empty my mind. Often I'd hear Mom's long, low whistle. I'd learned it was a special signal Kiko had taught her to call up shooting stars. Kiko came to visit, talk, and sometimes bring library books.

While I waited to execute the second part of my plan, the ocean part of my plan, I thought how piscina meant pool, fishpond, and baptismal font. I had this artificial ocean – the water, the waves, and the breeze, but no fish. Eventually, my plan was for Mom and me to travel back to Xihuatanejo – to the place of women. We'd carry Faith's ashes there and scatter them beneath the waves. The waves and their rhythms would breathe life back into Faith and into Mom and me. Together we'd travel the passages, canyons, tunnels, and archways of the coral reef and watch the many reef dwellers create their own peace. We'd model ourselves on the damselfish and its cousins, fish that lived among the anemones and took the anemones' name as theirs. We'd learn to survive among the venomous tentacles of the anemones. We'd learn like the damselfish and their cousins to find shelter where other marine life would be killed or paralyzed.

Faith's encyclopedia said coral – the limestone skeleton with its bright polyp anemones, animals masquerading as flowers – was the bridge between the plant and the animal worlds. The image I'd carried away from my one day on the coral reef was that of an underwater universe where colours were more vivid, shapes more surreal, and sounds more swollen with energy than in the universe I knew, maybe to compensate for the partial deadening of senses: sight, hearing, smell, touch. A world in which the inhabitants had learned to celebrate their difference: to see with their flanks, smell through their scales, taste without contact, and translate the electric charges of other beating hearts. A medium, as I saw it, that through my art might be used to bridge the physical and the spiritual.

So I began to make my own reef on the waiting canvas. And carve wooden moons and stars to hang in the secret compartments behind the false front. I soon discovered that Sonnie could only stay put watching me in the studio for an hour at a stretch. And only then if I'd taken her on her walk first. So after her morning bath, I settled her in her stroller and set out with my backpack. I slipped in a sketchbook, a box of charcoal, and an eraser to practise with alongside the diapers, blanket, toys, and bottles. I even had a folding stool.

When we got to the park, I spread out the blanket, laid Sonnie on her back and played with her a while, or watched as she explored her toys with her fingers, her eyes, her mouth. Then when some of the children came closer from the playground as they always did, I sat back and quicksketched them while they fingered Sonnie's rattle and touched her toes and hair. Their mothers came over to see my sketches. And walked away with their favourite of the drawings resting on the palm of their hands, careful not to spoil their child's likeness with a smudge or a fingerprint.

When mass ended and the church doors opened, the strains of music and voices in unison wafted over the square.

One or two parishioners got into the habit of stopping by to watch over my shoulder, until one day I asked if they'd like to pose. Doña Elisa was the first to take me up on my offer. She sat stiffly on the folding stool, until I put Sonnie in her lap.

Doña Elisa was the woman I'd followed into the church thinking she was Sor Rosario. The one who, like me, had brushed tears away at the end of mass. Maybe that was the need my occasional church-going met. To be surrounded by fellow sufferers, one of whom had been nailed to a cross.

Although I didn't want payment, the mothers of the children and the church-goers I sketched started leaving me little personal treasures in exchange for the drawings I gave away. Every treasure – every amulet, charm bag, birchbark bookmark, or miniature doll – was like a seashell that held each person's ocean in its curves.

I was rediscovering how to let an image make its way from a subject to my wrist again. Now, though, I drew from the outside only. Inside still hurt too much. In the exchange of paper for memorabilia, it was as though these other people with their stories helped me pull the spike from my chest and file it down to more manageable nails. Sharing nails the way people in another time shared loaves of bread. The pain of a bed of nails much easier to stand than that of a single spike.

I kept the sketches on the steamer chest in my bedroom and the mementoes in a plastic box I bought at the corner store when I realized I needed a system if I didn't want to end up confusing which person gave me what. My box looked like a plastic see-through pill box, but instead of having only seven small compartments, it had over thirty over-size ones; I wondered what kind of hypochondriac would ever need that many pills. Until I read the label: it was a sewing box for buttons. I wished there was someone to share the joke with. Maybe Faith was laughing with me even as the thought crossed my mind. Laughter tinged with bitterness that I had entertained the thought she might be a hypochondriac even as a tumour decided her fate.

José brought the box into the studio one day while I was working on the fish mural. He asked what the box was for, and I explained.

He said, "Now that's what you should be making into a fresco instead of the fish. All these faces and memories could add up to a masterpiece."

Maybe so. But for now, what I liked above anything else was that the sketches and trinkets had no purpose; all they represented was an exchange of gifts and shared trust.

Maybe the best art comes from the place where the artist and model meet. I no longer forced on these people – whom I didn't see as models – my vision of what they should be, or worried about the effect my muse might have on them or what the muse was telling me. Drawing Faith, my art had frightened me, it took me places I'd never been, showed me sights I should never have seen, and told a future I didn't want for her or me.

I used to think I had control. Of my art. Of my life. I was wrong.

I controlled nothing, not my art, not my life, not the pain. So now I let the space between us, between myself and these old people, these children and these mothers, decide what we gave and define the only image I conveyed. I met them somewhere in between.

José wouldn't let the idea drop. "Well, when I move in, I'm going to build you a frame ten times the size of this one. You'll need it, you'll see."

I had no explanation for the need to keep going back to the journal, Mom's journal now. It was almost like an addiction.

The need to smoke, the need to drink, the need to know. If questioned about an addiction, José might say mine, if any, was to drink. He didn't understand how a drink is like medication for a hurt no doctor diagnosed. But he'd be wrong. I didn't crave like a drunkard just one more swig. Or strain to hear the bottle calling to me wherever it hid. I craved just one look instead. In the journal. There was no ignoring its call.

Sometimes I think I've built a diver's cage with shark-repellent bars coated in want, love, and loss in which I have trapped you. Consecrating your ashes to the ocean would be, to me, like throwing away the key to the lock. But that's what Hope wants us to do.

She's still drawing you, she just hasn't recognized it yet. She paints angel fish, anemones, medusas, sea peaches, squid, and purple sea fans then creates doors from her underwater wonders behind which she hangs or glues the moon, the sun, and the stars. She thinks what we saw off the seashore together is the heaven you've found. She's wrong. But if she should happen to be right, that makes it even worse. Her underwater heaven is too fragile, as fragile as its coral depressions that shelter millions of lifeforms. She doesn't remember what happened that day she discovered the reef, how she panicked the first time she tried snorkelling without a life vest, how her legs dropped, and her flippers hit coral rock. Just one kick or two. But enough. A quarter of the world's reefs have been destroyed already by such a touch when untouched they could have lived for over a thousand years. A simple touch can extinguish thousands of lives: polyps and plants and the marine life they feed. If Hope is right and the reef is heaven, maybe my job is to ensure we don't transform her heaven into hell.

For the first time, I dreamt of holding Sonnie in my arms – Sonnie, not you, Faith. I rubbed my face against hers, only to see blood bubbling and wounds appearing on my cheek. Is it true that a fountain of blood is the spirit coming to life again, like new light against the darkness? I have no faith in the fragility of interpretation or of the reef.

I don't see the same fragility in the stars. I see infinity. The stars.
The skies. Scanning them for you Faith, for Pedro. For permission
to start over again.

In the church your sister has found a go-between, between the
world and beyond. Pedro chose to cut all ties, Hope has decided to
create new ones. I've lost faith in the go-betweens.

I wanted to tell my mother she was wrong. About the
reef at least. A reef is not broken forever. Coral polyps *can*
regenerate from broken pieces, soft tissues *do* start to grow
along the line where breakage occurred. And even before the
coral is given new life, there are plants and animals capable of
living on coral that has died. A reef was not as fragile as she
thought, maybe neither was she. But then again. The priest
spoke of how a man must be broken to find God. But did
God always find every broken woman and man, that was the
question I had.

I needed so badly to talk to someone about what my
mother wrote, but who? Not José. In Spanish, privacy is
intimidad. Couched in José's language, I saw my actions for
what they were. By reading words meant to remain intimate,
I had violated Faith's trust, my mother's trust. Violación.
Unforgiveable.

I was beginning to see how the unspoken words could
start to accumulate like sandbags between my lover and me.
The growing pile of sandbag upon sandbag gradually cutting
off communication between the two of us. I had done this
to myself. I had no one else to blame. But I kept reading.
Self-medicating. Staving off the worst.

.

XXII

Kiko came down with José the night before Mardi Gras. Kiko didn't show the same reticence toward José as toward me. Maybe José was excused for having been born into his faith, and it was the choosing Kiko couldn't understand. As usual, Kiko climbed up to the roof on arriving, sat there with my mother – he'd told José they sometimes didn't exchange a single word – then climbed back down. Kiko maintained that all grandmothers are fountains of teaching and that Sonnie's grandmother's teaching came with a stillness that was almost deafening. He was right. Just her written words had my ears ringing.

Before he came down again, José and I brought out extra chairs for the poolside. As I lugged my chair and watched José carry his, he turned and looked over his shoulder, "I did what you asked and contacted the Consulate. You have to come back to Mexico City with me after the holiday. I've made you an appointment with the visa office and then with the Mexican authorities. It will only take two days. We'll leave Sonnie with your mother."

I caught my breath. I hadn't thought this far ahead. Leave Sonnie? With my mother? Given everything I'd read about how she felt? My mother had barely enough strength to look after herself. How could we ask her to look after somebody else? After Sonnie? What if something happened to her? I

wanted to tell José, but how could I? It would mean telling him
I had read my mother's journal. That I had violated her trust.

José wasn't expecting an answer anyway. As far as he was
concerned, I was going.

For the first time ever, my mother came out with Kiko
and joined us beside the pool. Kiko preceded her down the
ladder, then squinted up from the bottom, holding one hand
out to steady her descent. José went looking for an extra
chair and brought us each out a beer.

José held out his bottle, mouthed "Arriba, abajo, al centro,
adentro," our unofficial toast, and took a gulp. Then Kiko said,
"José, I forgot. Would it be all right if I borrowed your car
sometime this week? Doña Ramona and I are going to go out
into the country to watch the skies, away from all the lights."

José gave a mock frown. "Hmmm. All that sky-watching
could be dangerous, you know."

Kiko raised his eyebrows with a smile. "What are you
talking about?"

"Look at Galileo. He was forever studying the sky – said
it taught him what questions to ask – and look where it got
him. He was threatened with death because too many people didn't like the questions he found there."

José and Kiko had grown close the way men do, comfortable teasing each other and letting down their guard. José
once told me his first reaction on seeing any other man was
to size him up and decide if he could take him on. José!

Watching them, I fell more in love with José than ever.
Papi severed his relationships with his friends first, then with
us. Maybe it was all part of following in Buddha's footsteps,
cutting off all ties with this life. I still wished he had spent
more time being human and forgotten about imitating some
sage.

"Sure, and you know who it was threatened him with
death, too, don't you? The Church. Lucky for us, it doesn't
have that kind of power today."

In the house, Sonnie squealed. She must be awake. I hated
to have to leave right then. On my way inside, I thought about
all the discussions that could be fueled with the Church's contradictions. José had told me once of one churchman, more
honest than the rest, who used to say pray as if you believed
in God. I guessed it meant I could be contradictory, too. That
I could love going to the occasional mass, but not convert.
That I could prefer a hand on my forehead and peace for my
mind's eyes to a sharing of the host. All I knew for sure was
that, if I had ever thought about it in the past, I assumed a
church had to be perfect, not like a life's companion or a
child, and that only a perfect church could ever be my companion on life's road. But now it seemed to me a church, with
its imperfections and contradictions, was very much like a life
companion or a child. The Church was other people. For the
longest time I didn't think I needed people. I'd thought I
could do it alone. I was wrong. I needed all dear enemies.

Sonnie broke into a smile when I bent over her crib. The
muscle that was my heart contracted so hard it hurt. It was a
miracle it could withstand this much love.

I had her changed and into the stroller in no time.
Holding the beer I'd forgotten to leave outside and accom-
panied by the squeaking front wheels, I maneuvered the
stroller over to the pool.

José came and unhinged the knee-high gate for me. If we
still lived here when Sonnie was learning to walk, that gate
would definitely need to be built up. I put the stroller under
the shade of a banana tree. Sonnie was content to spin the
plastic toys on her seatbelt, whisper "Ajá," and listen to the
sound of her own voice.

The other three sat in silence. The bantering mood of
minutes earlier seemed to have vanished. Each was lost in his
or her own thoughts.

Silence came easily to Kiko. He didn't speak unless he
had something to say.

It was my mother who finally said something, softly, as though thinking aloud to herself, a pause between each word. "I… didn't… know… life… could… be… this… hard."

None of us said anything at first. I felt a lump forming in my throat. Then Kiko said, so softly I wasn't quite sure I'd heard him right. "I knew it could be this hard. I just didn't know it would."

Funny how you can get so caught up in your own pain that you forget how it must translate for others. I didn't know why Kiko's response should surprise me. The bond between him and my mother seemed so obvious right now; they were each other's echo. In losing Faith, they had both lost their future, Mom her eldest daughter, Kiko, his lover and perhaps, some day, the mother of his child. The lump in my throat grew bigger, multiplied five-fold, for all of us sitting there, for our loss.

If ever there was a time for Faith to send us a sign, it was now. To show she was with us. If ever there was a time for Faith to send me a sign, it was now. Now that José was asking me to trust that I could leave Sonnie with our mother.

The four of us sat there, staring at the unspeaking waters of the pool.

A dragonfly flitted over the pool's expanse then stopped, hovering, halfway across. I watched its neon body, its wings looking much too fragile to defy gravity.

As we watched the dragonfly hover, its wings suddenly stopped beating as it tilted forward and plunged into the water without a sound. Seconds later, a lifeless body floated to the surface, flanked by wings forever stilled.

I felt like I had just witnessed a suicide. Me looking for signs, and this was the sign I'd been given. I thought I was going to be sick.

Kiko's voice held quiet surprise. "El caballito del diablo!" he said. Then he started to laugh. His laughter came from deep in his chest; it was rich, rolling, and alive.

After a second's hesitation, José stammered out, "Goo… good riddance to a bad ride!" His laughter paired up with Kiko's. I looked from one to the other until José took pity on me. "Ca… caballito del diablo, another word for dragon-fly."

Caballito del diablo. The devil's steed. A devil drowned.

That day when Faith told me about Papi talking from the other side, she said she never recognized the sign right away. Maybe the understanding of signs comes with a time lag, like a bad phone connection. How many signs were there out there I never heard for having stopped listening too soon?

I smiled at the two men, helplessly howling by now, my mother oblivious, still off in her own world, then I walked over to where Sonnie sat, her bottom lip trembling. Too much noise for a baby girl to take in.

Maybe there was a devil, who knows, and the caballito did just ride him to his death. If so, good riddance as José said. Or maybe it was only a dragonfly that mistook the pool for the ocean and its waters for heaven like me. Or maybe the devil had just been baptized.

Sonnie came gladly into my arms. In the safety of my embrace, she found the courage to stare at the roaring men. She looked back at me, then snuggled her head into the crook of my neck.

I kissed the soft spot on her crown and felt it pulse.

XXIII

Kiko and my mother left at 8 on the night of their outing. José and I fell into bed shortly after we put Sonnie
in her crib, around 9, both of us exhausted from Mardi Gras
the night before and the day's fast, but I couldn't sleep. I kept
thinking this would be my last chance to read my mother's
journal before José and I left for the city. Before we left without Sonnie. I tried to talk myself out of prying and dredge
up reasons for not repeat-offending, but nothing worked.
There were just as many reasons why I should. Sonnie, the
dragonfly, my mother's own words, Faith. Papi.

I slid out of bed without disturbing José, shrugged on a
robe, and slipped into Faith's huaraches.

My mother's journal was open face-down on her bed.

On the wall facing me, a wall that had always been
empty, my moon sketch of Faith was hung, the gold glitter-
ing in the reflection of the real moon's light. I sat down and
switched on the bedside lamp.

I had to flip back two then three pages to find the beginning of the entry showing that day's date. My mother's handwriting was jagged, almost illegible in places. I'd never seen
it this bad.

*Kiko talked me into going to Mardi Gras. Said if I'm ready to
make a trip out into the country, I'm ready for my first trip out of*

the compound. That's my name for the language school, my home. A compound. Hope called the evening a return to ordinary times. Which it wasn't, since the whole point was to celebrate Mardi Gras.

I'd forgotten about noise, people, the world outside. I'd forgotten about cascarones, Hope didn't know what they were. I bought four for the five of us. Cracked the first one on José's head to show her what it was about. Hoping the whole time a real egg hadn't been slipped into the lot. Smiled to watch her eyes go wide as I held the egg above his head then her laughter as the fine gold flour trickled out. Kiko was next. When I did Hope she closed her eyes. Fine gold dust sprinkled through her hair. I cracked the egg on my knuckles first for Sonnie; I wouldn't risk it on her fragile skull. I cradled the two broken halves in my hand, took a pinch of fairy dust to sprinkle on her head, and dumped the other half over myself. Sonnie laughed and laughed, a laugh that echoed in her tiny chest. Hope said, "And she saw that it was good," and I let her.

You know that life is hell when waking up is the real nightmare.

I woke to a marked daughter and grandchild. A black, ugly jagged cross etched on each of their foreheads where last night there'd only been my gold dust.

The God I know only gives to take away.

A priest placed the mark on her. Ash Wednesday, how could I forget? Ashes to ashes, dust to dust. I feel like now the truth is out. We have always been marked as prey. Every last one of us. Pedro, Faith, me, and now Sonnie and Hope.

I see myself, pistol in hand, picking off strangers one by one. Occasionally a god. Click! Click! Click! I thought I was strong. Strength has turned mean. Or weakness turned bad. But I know who each stranger really is. Myself. Every time my mind wanders to Faith's last days, those last hours, a gun materializes in my hand. I feel the cold metal trigger beneath my finger. Click. The gun jerks in my palm. I am the one I assassinate day in, day out. Click. Click. Click. But I'm safe as long as the muzzle aims away. Click. Click. Click. The image my censors hold back never comes up, the barrel against my own temple.

I won't let the gun turn against me. But why? That's the question I ask the stars. Because death is not a gift, they say. Then add, let there be light. I see no guns in the sky.

Now I remember why I stopped talking. Because I had no words for this wrath. The wrath that follows sorrow and guilt.

Guilt masks anger. My anger has been unmasked. So this is where madness is born, Pedro, I never knew. Suffering doesn't make you stronger, just more vulnerable to pain.

My mind has become a shooting gallery. I am a "huerfana de hija," an orphaned mother, and I have but one desire, to shoot.

This was what addiction felt like. This churning in the gut like half-digested poison.

I closed the journal, panicked, flipped it open again, else she'd discover I'd been reading it when she got back.

Now I knew why my mother spoke so little. Because her words were too brutal to be heard. She too gone mad. Going mad. It served me right.

My whole body was shaking, I had to make my way back down the ladder somehow, but my limbs didn't want to obey me. I put one foot in front of the other as far as the edge of the roof. One moment of clumsiness, and I'd be at the bottom without touching a single rung. I didn't move at first, just stood there knees bent, both hands resting on my thighs fluttering up and down. Gradually the shaking subsided, and I could move my feet.

I was a kid again, an abandoned daughter, with a secret too big to tell. I knew too much. I'd read too much. My mind had recorded words that were never meant to be there. Words on a page converted into voices in my head, sometimes my mother's, others Faith's, sometimes Papi's. I heard voices and they weren't the voice of God. I didn't know how to erase them, rewind them, or fast-forward over them. They were there to stay.

I slipped into bed, my back to José, who reached out half-asleep to draw me in closer. I made sure not to touch my head to his hand lying on my pillow. He mustn't feel the tears that had started to leak onto my cheeks. "What's wrong?" he murmured anyway.

I swallowed once, to clear a passageway, then said in my steadiest whisper, "Nothing. Why?"

His voice didn't sound as sleepy this time. He flattened his hand against my stomach. "Whenever you're sad, every muscle in your belly tenses up, like this." He pulled me in even closer, then reached up and felt my tears.

The decision had been taken from me. I had to tell him; his fingers like those of a blindman, read me as though my emotions had been punched out in Braille.

I turned to him, the poison flushing out. I told him about the cockroaches, Faith's papers, my recycled sketchbook, Sonnie. José didn't stop caressing me until there was nothing left to tell. If he felt disgust it never showed.

"It's only been three months," was all he said, "the shock is wearing off." José defending my mother. Another surprise. "The writing is part of the cure. They are only words. You don't need words, your mother's words. You should know that."

Should I? Who knows what's right or wrong, what's true or false? What about me, the good I haven't done, does that count, José? Violación. "I… the journals…"

José rolled away from me, onto his back. I was right to begin with, he could never forgive me. "How can I say? Life… it's like the ocean, but you, you treat it like an aquarium. It isn't. You don't decide what fish to populate it with, how much to feed them, what temperature the water should be, what plastic plants or fake plaster bridges or reefs to add. You're not in control."

My half-sob sounded pathetic even to my own ears. "I couldn't even get an aquarium right."

"What do you mean?"

"Back in Montreal. The goldfish we started out with. Then the frogs. The spring peeper."

"So, ya basta. Just stop."

The slow agonizing death in the lizard's mouth of that one tiny frog wearing an X on its back. An X like a cross. Suddenly, Papi's voice came to me, reading out the Latin name for peeper. He'd given up on finding such a frog in the Spanish-speaking world. *Pseudacris crucifer*. Pseudo-Christ crucified. Could my mother be right? That each of us was marked in our family, that we bore a God-given curse. That madness or illness was inevitably our lot?

But if I believed that, where would it lead? To more of the charlie-horse fear that buckled my knees and lanced my gut. I realized fear like this had to be tamed. Like the damselfish cousins that dwell among the anemones, I had to brush up against fear and its poison tentacles slowly, carefully, a little bit at a time until my body learned to adjust, to secrete the mucus that would prevent the anemone from discharging its poisonous sting.

I had to learn not to be paralyzed. To live with the fear that paralyzes was no way to lead a life. Nor was it a legacy to leave a child. Fear like that led nowhere.

José was right. I knew I had to stop. Already back on the roof I knew I would stop. I never again wanted to be in a place where I felt I had to set secret wrongs right. Only now I realized something else. The answer was to stop... and then go on from there. Everything could just stop here, then start anew. Stopping didn't mean paying penance, laying blame, suffering guilt. It just meant stop. Stop then go.

The image of my mother teaching me to dive when we snorkelled together those centuries ago surfaced. She made sure I'd mastered swimming and snorkelling without the aid of a life vest first, and then she taught me to dive. Scissor of legs straight up like a corkscrew to give me enough momentum for the plunge. She told me to take the snorkel out of my mouth, that way, instinctively, I would keep my mouth closed. A natural reflex. After a couple of dives, I thought I knew better. I'd rather keep the snorkel in and just hold my breath. But that turned my instincts off. At the bottom I inhaled through the tube without thinking, swallowed water, plankton, and who knows what else, and coughed all the long way back up. Coughing and hacking and spluttering to get the excess fluid out. When it could have been so easy.

With his arm still cradling my neck, José pulled me over gently so my head lay on his chest, "It's late, Esperanza. Let's go to sleep. Here, listen to my heart."

His heartbeat was regular, steady and sure. Ja–ja, ja–ja, ja–ja. A heartbeat required no response. With nothing asked of me, I surrendered to sleep.

My last wakeful moment was for Sonnie. When she is old enough, I thought, I will buy her a diary with a lock and key. I'll have her keep the key on a chain around her neck so the words she writes will be for her eyes only. I would always doubt myself. The temptation would always be there. But mostly I would ask her to for her own peace of mind. A journal for a girl on the path to womanhood. I promised myself that, unlike my mother and father, I would be there for the girl and the young woman she would become. Maybe I'd make her a journal myself, with quotes in calligraphy at the top of each page, and have a locksmith add the lock.

The first quote came to me unbidden then, on the crater's edge of sleep, like a gift or a sign or a bright burst of lava. It was this. So faith, hope, love remain, these three; but the greatest of these is love.

Acknowledgements

My heartfelt thanks go out to my family: my parents Lois and Jack Muir, my husband Joël, my beloved daughter Christelle and son-in-law Don Bender, and my cousin BJ Holliday – the sister I never had. Special thanks go out to my writer friends Barb Scott and Nancy Richler for their sage advice, to my artist friends Teri Posyniak, Susana Wald, Danielle Bianchetti, and Colleen Philippi for their inspiration, and to all my friends whose friendship has carried me through good times and bad. I would like to express my gratitude to the writing community for the encouragement and guidance I have received over the past twelve years, starting with Darlene Barry-Quaife, Fred Wah, Paul Quarrington, Roberta Rees, Richard Harrison, Ven Begamudré, Julie Johnston, Michèle Marineau, Nicole Markotic, Aritha van Herk, Bonnie Burnard, Mike Bryson, Richard van Camp, the University of Calgary creative writing classes, writers with the Markin-Flanagan Distinguished Writers Program, and the Sage Hill Writing Experience. I would also like to thank the Alberta Foundation for the Arts for giving me my start, and Rhonda Bailey and André Vanasse of XYZ who believed in me whether I translated or wrote. Finally, this novel is dedicated to the loving memory of my youngest daughter Katie, my brother Dan, and my grandmother Irene. You are with me always.